Darker

Musings

David Boiani

Foundations Book Publishing Company
Brandon, MS 39047
www.foundationsbooks.net

Darker Musings
By: David Boiani

Cover by: Dawné Dominique
Edited and formatted by: Steve Soderquist
Stevesoderquist.com
Copyright 2019© David Boiani

Published in the United States of America
Worldwide Electronic & Digital Rights
Worldwide English Language Print Rights

ISBN-13: 978-1-64583-000-9

Acknowledgements

Thanks to everyone who made Darker Musings possible. Also, as always to my readers, thank you for your support.

Dedication

For Leah...

Dedication

Table of Contents

THE STORM

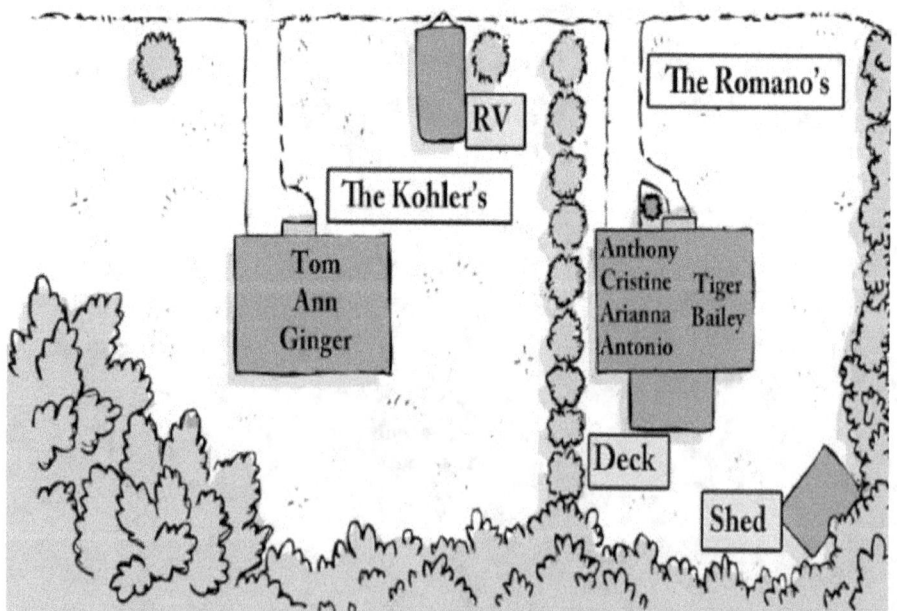

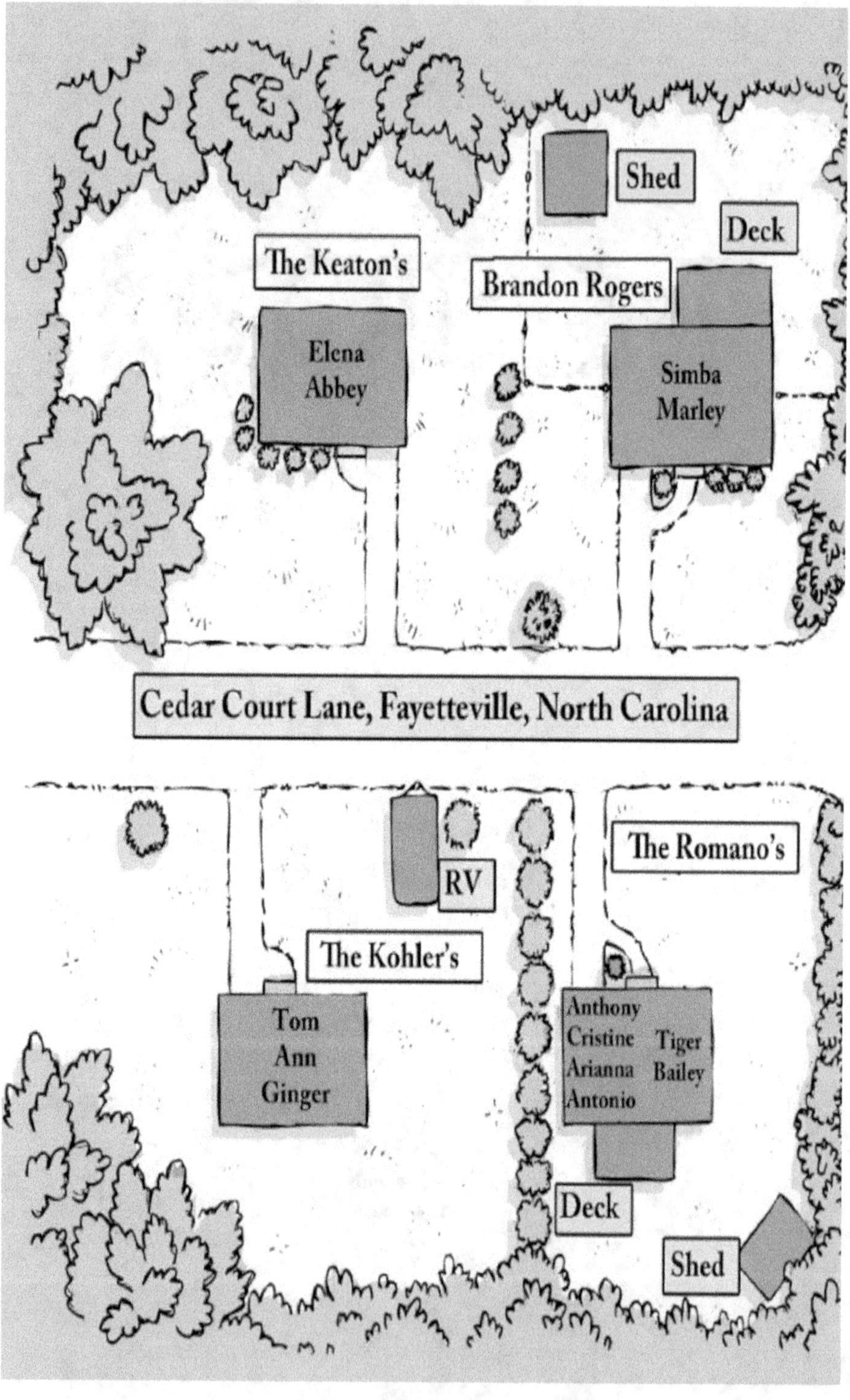

The Keaton's

Elena
Abbey

Shed

Deck

Brandon Rogers

Simba
Marley

Cedar Court Lane, Fayetteville, North Carolina

RV

The Romano's

The Kohler's

Tom
Ann
Ginger

Anthony
Cristine   Tiger
Arianna   Bailey
Antonio

Deck

Shed

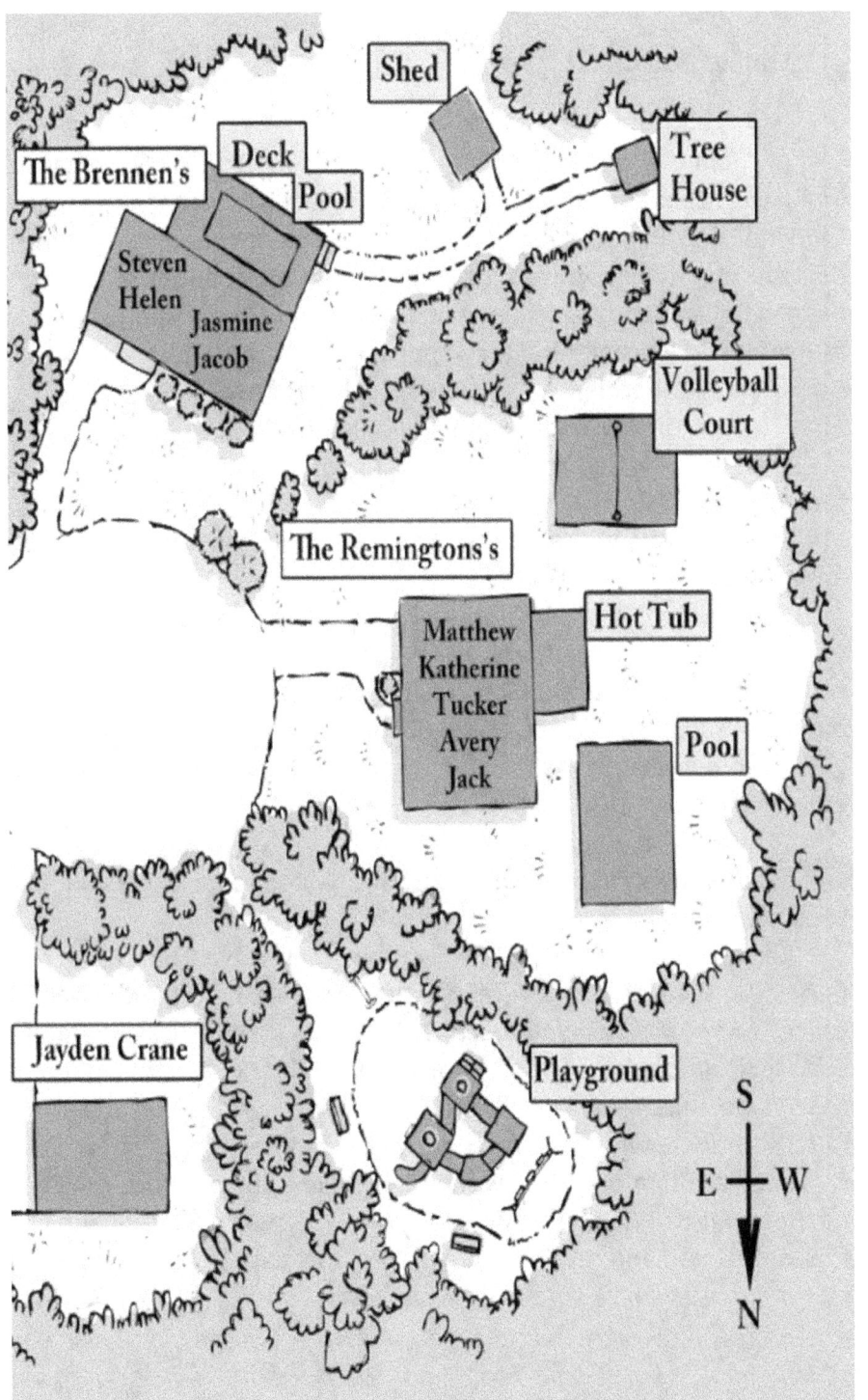

Friday, 9:30 pm...

Anthony waited in the playground holding Bailey's leash as the luminescent, full moon shone down from its high perch in the North Carolina sky. Bailey squatted just as Anthony heard Katherine's delicate footsteps approaching on the crushed stone path. Anthony bagged Bailey's droppings and placed them into the garbage can just as he noticed her beautiful face appear.

"Hello, Katherine," he said, moving toward her.

"Hi, Anthony, we can't keep doing this."

"Can't we? If you truly didn't want to you wouldn't have come tonight."

"This is crazy, we're both married with children and our families are at stake."

"Do you love me?" Anthony asked, looking into her eyes.

"I'm not answering that question. It's irrelevant."

She flinched as Anthony pulled her body in and their lips met in a bundle of fury. She hesitated and pulled away for an instant but then gave in to her desires. As their tongues danced, she recoiled from his embrace.

"Anthony, stop!"

"I can't get enough of your lips, baby. I need to be inside you. You send me off into a crazy state."

Katherine looked up at him wrapping her arms around his thick neck. "Okay, tomorrow afternoon. He'll be working on a case at the office. Tucker has baseball practice, Avery has gymnastics, and Jack is spending the day at a friend's house. Two o'clock...but Anthony, we have to be quick."

"Katherine, with you I can hardly help but be quick."

She gave him one last kiss and her sexiest smile before reaching down to pet Bailey. The moon shone in her eyes as she took one last look at the man and retreated down the short path toward her house.

David Boiani

Friday, 9:30 pm...

Abbey Keaton read the closed caption pass on the bottom of the screen as the young man spoke to the beautiful woman on the bow of the immense passenger steamship. Her mother, Elena, was in the kitchen making popcorn. Friday night was the Keaton's movie night and Abbey had requested "Titanic."

Elena walked into the room, handing an overflowing bowl of popcorn to her daughter as she sat down next to her.

"What did I miss?" she spoke in sign language.

"Thank you. The young man seems to be talking the pretty girl out of jumping overboard," Abbey replied.

"Really, how sad. Wow, he's a cute one, isn't he?" her mom said, referring to the handsome, young artist named Jack.

Abbey rolled her eyes at her mother and smiled. Elena laughed, pulled her daughter in and kissed her on the forehead. Abbey smiled and said, "I love you, mom."

Friday, 10:00 pm...

Marley and Simba vigorously waged their tails as Brandon walked them down Cedar Court Lane. The sun had set over an hour ago as the bright, full moon shone down. He passed the Kohler's to turn onto Fairview Drive and stopped to look at Kohler's motor home parked in the front yard. He'd always admired the vehicle and the excellent shape the retired couple had kept it in. Brandon hoped when he retired he would have an RV of his own and take his children's families on vacation. He yearned to make up for lost time since his wife, Morgan, left him and took their children to Raleigh. Steve, Brandon's twenty-year-old son, was home from Duke University for the summer. Ashley, Brandon's seventeen-year-old daughter lived with her mother full time.

Brandon started down Fairview and the happy canines walked alertly by his side. The night was calm and pleasant with a haunting stillness that seemed magical. Simba and Marley sniffed the air and looked up at the sky as their instincts detected something approaching. Something unique. Something sinister. Something violent.

Friday, 10:05 pm...

"Ann, Brandon is checking out Bertha again," Tom Kohler said as he glanced out of his bay window at Brandon Rodgers. A feeling of empathy came over him as Brandon stopped with his dogs in tow to inspect the Kohler's motorhome.

"Aw, he's such a nice man. One day I hope he gets his own, he deserves it."

"Maybe one day we can give it to him when we upgrade to Bertha the second."

"Tom, that's so sweet. You're so thoughtful and caring, that's why I fell in love with you so long ago."

"Really? I thought it was my magnetic masculinity."

"Well, yes, sure, that too," she replied. She walked up to her husband and reached her arms around him as they watched the lonely man march down the street with his dogs and turn onto Fairview Drive.

"That man fought for this country and rushed into burning buildings to save the lives of people he didn't even know. Gifting Bertha to him is the least we could do," Tom said. Ann smiled and put her head on his shoulder as Brandon moved out of their sight.

Friday, 10:30 pm...

The deep ruby liquid sloshed around the wine glass as Steven Brennen took another sip of Cabernet. He kept the wine in his mouth savoring the earthy, smoky, fruity flavor while he scanned the Daily Fayetteville Observer. Helen slid in his lap and put her arms around his neck hoping to garner some of the interest away from the newspaper.

"Put that away, Doctor Brennan. This is my time," she said with a sexy smile, lightly brushing her lips against his.

"Okay, you win," he replied, placing the paper on the table.

"Any interesting cases today, doctor?"

"Mrs. Brennan, you know that falls under the physician-patient confidentiality clause."

"Oh, really, does that mean I have to earn it?" she said as her hand slowly moved to the front of his pants.

"Maybe," he said, a playful smirk forming on his lips. "One is a young woman who's a borderline dissociative identity disorder patient, another, an older man who claims he hears voices of people from his past. Finally, a married woman who wears revealing clothes in public for attention. Any of these cases interest you?"

"Yes, the married woman. Why would she do such a thing?"

"She has esteem issues. She's addicted to attention, craves it."

"Does her husband know?"

"No, she's too humiliated to tell him."

"Have you helped her control it at all?"

"I hope so. I think so. She gets a rush from the attention. She's even resorted to flashing men at times. That's when she hit rock bottom and came to me for help. I've cured her of that practice, but she could relapse at any time. I make her aware of her accomplishments and her value as a human being. She's never sexually acted on these impulses to receive attention, but that's always a possibility if she doesn't fully recover. Sex is a common practice used by people who need to feel wanted or valued."

"That's so sad. So, Doctor Brennan, can I lay on your couch tonight? Maybe you can help make me feel physically and emotionally satisfied."

Steven smiled and he looked into his wife's big brown eyes. After all these years he still had an irresistible attraction to her.

"Are Jacob and Jasmine asleep?" he asked.

"Jacob is, Jasmine is in her room watching television and probably on her phone. She's been spending quite a bit of time texting our neighbor, Tucker. You need to keep an eye on that boy."

"Oh, I will. But first, you need your session. The doctor is in."

Friday, 11:45 pm...

Jayden sipped his scotch as the last scene he wrote settled in his mind. He placed his glass down and glanced at the screen. To kill or not to kill, that is the question. Sometimes characters die because it's an integral part of the plot. Sometimes they die because the author is still pissed off about getting cut off on the highway that day. That's just the reality of being a fictional character in a novel.

Jayden needed a break. He picked up his glass and walked out the back door to get some air. Writing can be exhausting at times, especially when there's a deadline to meet. Jayden built his house on Cedar Lane five years ago. Being an introvert and a loner, he preserved most of the surrounding trees to secure his privacy. People referred to him as a strange recluse, but he didn't care. He was happy in seclusion.

Jayden glanced up at the night sky, noticing electricity in the air. The full moon was especially bright as the glow illuminated the tops of the white pines surrounding his house. He took the last swig of his scotch and headed back inside. Bestsellers didn't write themselves, so he had a long night ahead of him.

Saturday, 6:00 am...

Matthew Remington woke to a wailing alarm clock, showered, and dressed. As he headed out, he stopped to look at his wife still asleep in their bed. The blankets hung off her body revealing the curve of her right hip and breast. She always slept in panties and a white t-shirt, a combination that Matthew found extremely sexy though he failed to inform her of that. The truth was something had changed between them over the years. The communication had broken down. He chose to put his work first and their relationship had weakened from that decision. Regardless, Matthew was a handsome, successful man who provided everything for his family. Surely Katherine understood that. For an instant, the vibrant glow of his wife's skin made him consider jumping back into bed and peeling those panties and t-shirt off his wife, but the thought faded as quickly as it had come. He had work to do, surely she understands that. He walked out, once again squandering a chance to save their relationship and marriage.

Saturday, 10:00 am...

The birds chirped in a chorus of melodies, promising a beautiful day forthcoming. Christina Romano listened to nature's songs as she sipped her first coffee. Tiger, her Maine Coon, rubbed against her legs as the rays from the sun danced through the treetops. She glanced up as Anthony walked out and sat next to her.

"Hi, baby, what are your plans today?"

"I have a few jobs to price and apply estimates for, but I'll be home later this afternoon," her husband answered while looking up at the sky.

"Driveways?"

"Yes, all driveways for private residences."

"Okay, I'm taking Arianna and Antonio to the mall to shop for school clothes."

"Already?" he remarked, finally focusing his eyes on her.

"Yes, I don't like to wait and then feel rushed in late August."

"Well, good luck. Are they sleeping?"

"Yes, the teen years are approaching."

"I'm going to wake them up," he said. Christina watched him walk back into the house. Her husband seemed to have grown a bit distant over the past year or so, however, his concrete business had boomed recently so she assumed his aloofness was a direct result of work overwhelming him. She took her last sip of coffee and headed back inside to pour another cup.

Saturday, 11:00 am...

The volleyball landed hard just inside the backline. Tucker retrieved it and positioned himself for the next serve.

"You're pretty good for a girl. I usually beat everyone pretty easily, but you're making me work."

"Um, thanks, I think. Sometimes I don't know whether to take your statements as insults or compliments," Jasmine said.

"Well, that was meant as a compliment. Did you fall asleep on me last night? I sent the last text at 11:00 and you didn't respond," Tucker replied as he spiked the ball past Jasmine and on the left boundary.

"That was out!"

"No, it was in, but I'll give you the point."

"No, I don't want a handicap. I can beat you straight up, mister."

"Okay," Tucker replied with a smirk.

"My mom checked on me. I pretended I was sleeping so she turned my TV off. I think her and my dad wanted to fool around so I went to sleep after she left my room."

"I understand, there're certain things we just shouldn't have to hear," Tucker said as he winked at his friend.

"Exactly," Jasmine replied as she noticed Tucker's dimples from across the court.

Saturday, 12:00 pm...

Katherine pulled out of her driveway, drove down Cedar Court Lane and turned south onto Fairview Drive with her three children in tow.

"What do you guys want for lunch?"

All three children howled different choices at the same time.

"Hold on, we'll take a vote. Everyone name their top two choices. Tucker?"

"Pizza, grinders."

"Avery?"

"Chinese, sushi."

Tucker's hands flew into the air at the thought of eating sushi as his sister glared at him. "Sushi? Really?"

"Tucker, you had your choice, Avery gets hers. Jack?"

"Cheeseburgers and fries, pizza."

"Sorry Avery, it looks like pizza," Katherine said.

"Whatever," Avery said with a disgusted look on her face.

Tucker laughed and pointed at his younger sister. He enjoyed getting his way, which had become commonplace for him. When you're a handsome, intelligent, athletic teenager, people seem to go out of their way to please you.

Katherine pulled her silver SUV into the Twisted Toppings Pizza parking lot. They picked a booth, ordered, and soon were downing two large pizzas loaded with toppings.

"Okay, troops, here's the plan. Drop Jack off at Jason's for 1:00, Avery at the gym for 1:30, and Tucker at the field for 1:45. Sound good?" Katherine looked around at the bright, young faces of her children as they stuffed pizza into their mouths. Nobody replied. "Great, let's finish eating and we're off."

Saturday, 1:00 pm...

Brandon pushed his lawnmower over the length of his front lawn before pausing for a moment to glance at the sky. Ominous looking clouds started to creep across the western sky, heading east. *Strange, the weatherman called for a sunny and pleasant afternoon,* he thought before continuing his work. Brandon liked to lose himself in manual labor at times. It was uncomplicated and rewarding, unlike dealing with people who can be complex and duplicitous at times, his ex-wife being case sample number one. He was the gentle, pleasant, straight-forward type but he also possessed a strong, stern, inner resolve and he wasn't afraid to speak his mind when the situation called for it.

As he finished his next pass he noticed his neighbor, Abbey, sitting on her front steps. He turned off the mower and walked over. As he approached, Abbey looked up at him and waved. He said, "Hello," in sign language.

"The dogs are in the backyard if you'd like to see them," he said. Brandon knew Abbey loved animals, especially his canines. She played with Marley and Simba every chance she had.

"Yes, I would love that," she replied. "Let me tell my mom," she said as she hurried inside.

Five minutes later she walked over and Brandon opened the gate for her to enter the backyard. The two dogs ran over to greet her, and she knelt to pet them as they excitedly waged their tails and licked her face. Brandon chuckled as he watched. He loved Abbey as if she were his own daughter and he'd do anything for her or her mother, Elena. The two dogs knocked her to the ground and covered her face with canine kisses as she laughed and hugged them both, bringing a broad smile to Brandon's lips.

Saturday, 1:55 pm...

Katherine pulled into her driveway, conflicted about what was about to happen. She was excited to feel the raw desire and emotion that Anthony extracted from her. It was a feeling that had been dead inside her for years and experiencing it again made her feel youthful and alive. However, she needed to end the affair. Too much was at stake. Anthony's touch had become drug-like to her and she hoped she was strong enough to end the relationship.

She parked her car and walked onto the deck to wait. He'd be here any moment and she fought to control the excitement rising in her heart and body. *I can't be in love with him,* she thought as her heart rate quickened from the anticipation of his touch.

Saturday, 2:00 pm...

Anthony parked his truck on Pine Ridge Street, south-east of Cedar Court Lane. His thoughts turned to making love to Katherine as he slowly made his way through the woods to Katherine's backyard. As he cleared the last of the trees he saw her waiting patiently on her deck. She heard footsteps approaching and her heart began to race.

"Hi beautiful," he said as he climbed the stairs.

"Hi," she replied.

David Boiani

He sat down next to her, put his arm around her waist and brought his lips to hers.

"Anthony, stop! We can't do this out here. What if someone sees us?"

"No one can see us in your backyard," he replied.

"You never know who may walk back here. I'm not worried about Mr. Crane, but one of the Brennen children? Jasmine has a crush on Tucker. What if she comes back here looking for him?"

"Okay, okay, you win," he said as he sat up and took his hands off her. "Let's go inside."

"Patience, mister. First, we need to talk. Anthony, this is the last time. I like you, I really do, but this is crazy and dangerous. My family means too much to me, as should yours. After today, it's over."

"Katherine, this is your decision. I can't make you continue this if you don't want it. If ending this is really what you want, I won't fight it."

Katherine smiled, grabbed his hand and said, "Follow me handsome."

Saturday, 2:00 pm...

Jasmine stepped out of the front door and walked to the mailbox to get the mail for her mother. She looked up suddenly as she heard footsteps in the woods behind the volleyball court in the Remington's yard. She glanced over and saw Mr. Romano walk out of the thicket towards the deck. *That's strange. What's Mr. Romano sneaking around Tucker's yard for?* That morning while playing volleyball with her, Tucker had mentioned he had baseball practice and that Avery and Jack would be out as well. Also, Mr. Remington worked every Saturday. As she thought about whether she should mention it to Tucker, her little brother, Jacob, ran out from the backyard.

"Jasmine, come out to the tree house with me. Jack's gone today and I have no one to play with."

"Okay, but only for a short while."

They walked into the backyard, down the short path covered by shrubbery, and into the woods to the tree-house their father had built for them when they moved in five years ago.

Saturday, 2:15 pm...

Katherine led Anthony to her bedroom. She relished the anticipation of making love to Anthony in her bed for the first time. She felt the blood pumping through her veins and her primal urges intensify with every step.

"Katherine, are you sure?"

"If this is our last time, I want it to be in a bed. Now kiss me."

Anthony took her in his arms and kissed her which sent a chill throughout her body. *Why does his touch make me feel this way?* she wondered. He ran his hand slowly up her thigh. Her skin tingled with expectation. He pushed her onto the bed and continued kissing her as his hand reached her inner thigh and under her sundress. He parted her thighs and felt the warmth emanating from her groin, just inches above his fingers. He slowly pulled her dress up around her waist as his fingers met her wetness. He stood up, his eyes connected with hers and undid his pants, letting them fall. She glanced down at the part of him she yearned for and watched as it grew.

"Anthony, I need you inside of me."

He smiled as he slid between her legs and they became one, a perfect fusion of passion and desire.

Saturday, 2:30 pm...

"Just one more game, Jacob," Jasmine said, sitting on the floor in the upper room of the treehouse.

"Okay, my deal," Jacob said as he dealt out the cards to play crazy eights.

"Oh, you're going to lose this time, mister."

Jacob paused as the wind outside picked up and the treehouse swayed slightly to the rhythmic gusts.

Saturday, 3:00 pm...

John watched as his two newborn babies wriggled in their bassinets. They each donned a small cap; the girl's pink and the boy's blue. They were the most beautiful sights he'd ever taken in. Suddenly there was movement from the corner of the room. Shadows danced and something shifted just outside of John's vision.

"Who's there?" John asked as he peered through the glass. He noticed what looked like a man's silhouette against the far wall move forward, toward the bassinettes which contained his babies. As the light reflected on the figure, he noticed it wasn't walking, but floating on air. He also realized it was no man. The creature had a man's face, but any human resemblance ended there. It sported two horns that spiral up above its head, beady red eyes, and ragged, black wings that fluttered behind it as it levitated across the room. Before turning its ugly head towards the babies, it looked straight at John and smiled, revealing a vile set of razor-sharp, jagged yellow teeth. John started screaming and pounding on the glass to no avail as it was impenetrable. He heard the newborns harrowing wails as their blood splattered on the floor, walls, and ceiling. The beast turned with a little foot hanging out of its mouth that it continued to chew until the extremity was gone. Blood covered its evil mouth and a long, black forked tongue protruded from the mouth to lick it up. John screamed and continued to pound on the partition. The creature floated slowly over to the glass and looked John in the eyes. With only a couple of feet between them, the beast threw its head back and let out the most chilling, evil laugh John had ever heard. John dropped to his knees with his face in his hands...

Jayden closed the book so he could absorb what he just read. He would often read books in his own genre to expand his mind, sharpen his craft, and learn new techniques. He'd started reading a book called *The Redemption,* which was recommended by his editor, Sharon.

Already halfway through, he admired the stark, gritty style it was written in.

He placed the book on the table and stepped out into the backyard. Looking up at the sky, he noticed a dark cloud cover starting to move in over Fayetteville, North Carolina. He felt a breeze kick up and noticed a slight drop in temperature. The goldfinches and blue jays were frantically flying around the trees and chirping as if they were troubled by a predator nearby. Jayden took in a deep breath and felt electricity in the air as it passed through his lungs. Something was approaching. Something uninvited. Something unpredicted.

Saturday, 4:00 pm...

As the sun slipped out of view, dark clouds moved in, covering the afternoon sky. The wind intensified and suddenly the feeling of a cool autumn day filled the air. Ginger, the Kohler's doxie, stuck her nose into the strengthening breeze as the trio passed Jayden Crane's house.

"Tom, it looks like a bad storm's moving in. Let's get back home before the sky opens up."

"Once Ginger does her business," Tom replied.

They continued around the circular end of the cul-de-sac, passing the Remington's, the Brennen's, and stopping at the small, wooded area at the side of Brandon's house. Tom picked up Ginger's droppings and they continued toward their house. The rain came as soon as they were safely home. It started lightly at first but quickly increased in intensity. They saw the first flash of lightning, followed by a small crack of thunder. Ginger ran into the bathroom to hide safely behind the toilet.

Saturday, 4:30 pm...

Brandon made it a habit to call his children every day to check on them and let them know he was thinking about them. Though he didn't love all the technological advances the world had made over the last ten years, one of the advantages was he could dial his children directly on their cell phones without talking to his ex-wife, Morgan. Their relationship had deteriorated to the point of even the slightest communication a challenge. He dialed his daughter's number and she picked up on the first ring.

"Hi, Daddy."

"Hi, baby girl. How are you today?"

"I'm good, was just on my way out."

"Where to? Not a date, I hope."

"Well, kind of. I met someone who goes to Duke. Steven knows him."

"Ashley, listen. You know I tease you about boys but I'm being serious now. Be careful. I trust you to make good decisions. When do I get to meet him?"

"Dad, this is our first date."

"Where are you going?"

"Pizza and bowling."

"Where?"

"Lucky Strikes Lanes."

"Okay, have fun, Ashley. Speaking of Steven, where is he? I left him a voicemail earlier."

"I think he has a date as well."

"If you talk to him tell him to give me a ring."

"I will, dad. I have to go finish getting ready now."

"Have fun, I'll call you tomorrow."

As Brandon hung up, he wondered where his innocent, young children went. It seemed that his children had become adults overnight. A dull ache shot through his heart as he thought back to a day years ago when he took them sledding. It was a rare snow day in Fayetteville. He was off from the station and school was canceled. At the time he didn't realize that memory would come back to him often, proving how precious time is. He'd give anything to live through just one more of those memories, but sadly, those times were gone forever. His eyes watered a bit as a hard rain started to fall outside.

The Storm

Saturday, 5:00 pm...

Anthony pulled into his driveway already missing Katherine's touch. What started as just sex had slowly turned into something more. Though he loved being with her, Anthony knew she was right, their affair was crazy and reckless. He knew it had to end, although his desire for her touch, her scent, her taste, overwhelmed him.

He stepped out of his truck into a downpour. The wind picked up and nearly blew him over as he quickly walked up the stairs to the front door and entered.

"Where have you been? I called three times," Christine said as she walked into the foyer.

"I know, I was talking to costumers. What is it with this weather? I thought it was supposed to be a beautiful weekend?"

"The weatherman just came on for a special report. He sounded like he didn't know what was going on, where the storm came from, or how long it'll last."

"Did you go to the mall? Where are the kids?"

"Yes, I called you on the way home. They're upstairs in their rooms."

Anthony turned as he heard a deafening crack of thunder followed by an immense flash that brightened the sky. A moment later, he looked out the bay window as the telephone pole in front of their house fractured and split in two. Half of it fell came crashing on his truck, just as the lights went out.

Saturday, 5:10 pm...

The purple sky opened and the wind whipped relentlessly as Katherine drove her three children home. Thunder roared followed by lightning that lit up the darkening sky.

"Mom, what the hell is going on?" Tucker asked.

"Don't swear, Tucker. I have no idea. The news said nothing of a storm moving in today."

"Mom, I'm scared," Jack said from the backseat as he started to cry. Trees were bent over, trash barrels were blown across the street, and minor flooding had started.

"Jack, toughen up will ya," Tucker said.

"Leave him alone," Avery said as she hugged her little brother.

"Everyone, relax. We'll be home soon. I'm sure this will pass quickly," Katherine said. Moments after those words left her mouth a large branch flew into the passenger side window, shattering it. Tucker jumped as the broken glass sprayed on and around him.

"Tucker!" his mother screamed. "Don't move!" He glanced at his mother with a look of horror on his face. "Don't worry, sweetie. When we get home I'll help you get out." Tucker's terrified eyes remained on his mother and Jack's crying intensified. The wind lashed against the vehicle as the rain poured into the open space left by the shattered window. Tucker was immediately drenched. What they saw next made them all realize this wasn't just another normal, innocent storm that would soon pass and be forgotten. Up ahead a tree had fallen over a small car, crushing the driver and passenger. Blood was splattered over the spider webbed windows. Katherine slammed on the brakes.

"Everyone, look away. You don't want to see this." She backed up and turned down a side street to take a different route home. The children were silent except for the soft whimpering of Jack's muffled sobs. Katherine glanced at her oldest. Tucker, her brave, proud son, had tears streaming down his face.

Saturday, 5:15 pm...

Brandon knew something was wrong. He gazed out his front window as Marley and Simba howled desperately by his side. He saw a flash and heard a loud crack from the street minutes before, prior to the electricity going out. He was now looking at the cause. The telephone pole in front of the Romano's house was destroyed, part of it having landed on Anthony's truck. As he peered out the window he noticed the trees bent over from the tremendous wind and watched as the hardest rain he'd even seen fell from the sky. Brandon knew this storm was something exceptional. Suddenly, his thoughts turned to his neighbors. He had to go next door and check on Abby and Elena.

Saturday, 5:20 pm...

Jayden stood in the middle of his small backyard as the rain soaked him and tremendous cracks of thunder accompanied by intense flashes of lightning rocked Fayetteville. *I am not afraid of you*, he thought as he raised his arms to the sky and turned his head up to accept the storm head on. His thoughts traveled back to one night, thirty-eight years ago...

Jayden was seven years old as a storm moved in. His parents had separated a few months prior and some days his mother worked late, leaving him alone after school. The thunder roared, the lightning lit up the house, and the rain felt like it would come straight through the roof. Anna, his mother, wouldn't be home for a few more hours. He crawled into his bed, pulled the covers over his eyes, and cried until the storm let up and his mother finally arrived home...

A deranged grin appeared on Jayden's lips as he stood, face to the sky, welcoming nature to attempt to frighten him now. The grin soon turned into a demented laugh as the thunder shook the ground around him and the continuous lightning brightened the sky.

Saturday, 5:30 pm...

The storm intensified as Matthew headed home. He picked up his cell to call Katherine but there was no service. He heard the rush of sirens as fire engines and rescues hurried to aid in the many accidents occurring throughout the town. It was then all the lights went out. Fayetteville was blanketed in a cloak of darkness. He threw his cell phone down and prayed his family was safe.

Saturday, 5:45 pm...

After a long, stressful drive, Katherine finally pulled up the driveway and into the garage. On the way home, they witnessed five people dead and many police cruisers, fire engines and rescue vehicles racing around to help people in distress. The town was a wreck with many already dead or injured.

"Avery and Jack, go inside. I need to pick up the glass around Tucker."

The children did as they were told. Katherine put on a pair of gardening gloves, opened the passenger door and proceeded to pick up the larger shards of glass. She scooped up what remained and put her hand on Tucker's shoulder.

"Okay, Tucker. Lift your legs and swing them out of the car. Do *not* slide on the seat. Push up with your arms and jump out."

Tucker followed her directions and moments later they were safely inside, rejoining Avery and Jack.

Saturday, 5:50 pm...

"Jasmine, where's Jacob!" Helen shouted as she entered her daughter's bedroom.

"He was in the tree-house a few hours ago."

"What? You left him there? He must be terrified!"

"When I left him, it wasn't raining yet. I'll go get him."

"No, I'll send your father. It's getting really bad out there."

Moments later, Steven walked out of the back door into a typhoon of wind and rain. A gust almost blew him over as he quickened his pace and headed down the path toward the treehouse. As he approached, he noticed the ladder was missing. All that remained were scattered pieces of wooden steps and rails on the ground.

"Jacob!" he yelled through the wind, rain, and thunder, hardly hearing himself. He looked up and noticed the lower room was destroyed. Two walls were blown completely off and the floor was tilted toward the ground. The top room, which was securely nestled between four thick branches was still intact. Steven knew his son was in that room, scared half to death. Steven turned and ran toward the house as the rain mixed with hail, pelting him on his head. He needed the aluminum extension ladder. He knew it was a risk, but he had no other choice if he wanted to save Jacob. He carried it down the path, praying the lightning would stay away. He reached the treehouse and secured the ladder in place. He quickly climbed the steps, crawled into what was left of the lower room, and pulled himself into the upper room. He found his son in the corner curled into a ball, crying. He crawled over and held him in his arms.

"It's okay, buddy, I've got you. Now let's get out of here."

They crawled out of the top room and stopped at the waiting ladder.

"You go first, I'm right behind you," Steven said.

He watched his son ascend the ladder and soon was following him down. Steven saw an immense flash of light and felt an intense charge enter and leave his body. His body burned as his clothes combusted. He was thrown thirty feet, landing in a thicket of shrubbery on his back. As he turned on his side, Steven Brennan's final vision was his eight-year-old son's body charred and lifeless. Then...blackness.

Saturday, 5:50 pm...

Brandon attempted to call Ashley but there was no service. He grabbed his windbreaker and pulled it on as he headed next door. He stepped out his front door and paused, noticing something strange. The wind had steadily increased since the storm moved in, but something a bit more worrisome was occurring now. The rain was changing, slowly transforming into a solid form. *Hail,* he thought, as he watched marble sized stones bounce off the pavement. The sky lit up as a flash of lightning hit down somewhere in the backwoods. The world was getting tossed around like a rowboat in open ocean waters. A crack of thunder shook the ground as he sprinted for the Keaton's front door. He knocked loudly and seconds later Elena opened the door.

"Brandon, come in! What the hell is going on?" Elena asked as Brandon rushed inside.

"Where's Abbey?"

"She is in her room, she's fine."

"Both of you should come and wait this out at my house."

"Okay, I'll get Abbey," she said as she hurried from the room.

Brandon escorted the ladies safely back to his house. All three were greeted happily by Simba and Marley as Brandon lit up a few candles and retrieved a few blankets for his guests. They all settled in the living room, warm and safe, as the storm continued to evolve and amplify.

Saturday, 5:55 pm...

Every route to Cedar Court Lane was blocked, either by a falling tree, downed telephone pole, or flooding. Matthew pulled over to wait out the storm. Hopefully a street would open up soon so he could get home. As Matthew glanced around at the carnage implemented by mother nature, he noticed something odd. There were no police cruisers, fire engines, town trucks, or rescues anywhere. Surely they should be out helping people or clearing the streets for safe passage. Did they all go home to be with their families? If so, what news did they receive that made them abandon their jobs? As Matthew sat back to relax a bit, the hail fell harder, the stones growing by the second. He heard them pound the roof of his car as he prayed the windshield would hold up to the battery.

Saturday, 6:00 pm...

"It's like nighttime out there already," Tom Kohler said as he stood by his picture window and monitored the street.

"It's two hours early. Tom, what's going on?"

"The storm's cloud cover must be so thick the sun's rays literally can't get through. It's getting colder by the second, too. The hail is getting heavier, with larger stones. Look at it, Ann."

Ann walked over, hugged her husband and watched with him as the barrage of solid precipitation continued. The wind picked up and the hail started to fall laterally, into the picture window.

"Tom, will it hold?" the rat-a-tat-tat of the hail hitting the glass resembled a machine gun wasting belt after belt of ammunition. Ginger, who'd been exploring the strange sound with her owners, now turned and ran into the bathroom, hopefully finding comfort and safety there. Suddenly, a small chink appeared in the glass, which quickly multiplied into many cracks, spreading out in every direction.

Tom pulled his wife back, away from the front of the house as the pane gave, inviting the elements in.

Saturday, 6:15 pm...

Helen was distraught. It had been a half hour since Steven headed to the treehouse to save Jacob. She stood with Jasmine, both looking out the back window waiting and praying for them to appear from the path. The intense rain had changed to hail which bounced off the decking and splashed down in the pool, making it seem as if it were boiling. Helen saw the flash of lightning touch down somewhere in the backwoods. Did it hit her husband and son? Or, were they still in the treehouse, waiting it out?

"I'm going back there to check on them," Helen said.

"No, Mom! It isn't safe. If someone is going, I am. It's my fault they're back there to begin with."

"Don't be ridiculous. Stay here and I'll be right back."

Before Jasmine could stop her, her mother darted out the back door and headed for the path as fast as she could as the golf-ball-sized hail battered her head. She fell to her knees as the onslaught continued, cutting her scalp and knocking her unconscious. Blood flowed from every gash as the flow of hailstones increased.

"Mom!" Jasmine screamed. She ran into Jacob's room and grabbed his batting helmet. The fit was tight, but she was able to force it on her head. She ran out the back door, immediately feeling the force of the hail pounding off the helmet. She approached her face-down, motionless mother and pulled her onto her back. Her mother was gone. Empty, glassy eyes looked back at her. She screamed and dropped her mother's body before turning and blindly running down the path. She felt the helmet crack from a hailstone the size of a cue-ball as she approached the treehouse. There was nothing left but pieces of shattered wood. She looked around, noticing her brother's body fifty feet from her. Smoke was still emanating from his flesh. She dropped to her knees and wept, ignoring the continued barrage of hail. She got to her feet and walked toward Jacob's body. Every step she took uncovered another body, her father's, just feet from Jacob. The air suddenly smelled like charred meat. She felt a fit of nausea overtake her, followed by a wave of vomit. Then the world went black.

Saturday, 6:20 pm...

Anthony glanced east, out of the living room window on the side of the house. The tan, sandstone color of Katherine's house occasionally came into view when an especially strong gust of wind sent the branches of the trees on his eastern property line into a frenzy. He hoped she was home and safe. He remembered she had to pick up her children, however, he didn't recall seeing her SUV return.

He thought about taking a walk over to check on her but with the mutant hail now falling and the daunting winds continuing to strengthen, he thought better of it. How would he explain it to Christina anyway? Anthony felt a bit puzzled by his feelings for Katherine. At first, it was a connection driven by lust, but over time it became something much more, something Anthony could no longer control. He wasn't comfortable with anyone having power over him as Katherine did.

"Is it starting to break at all?" Christina asked as she approached him from behind.

"No, it's actually getting worse. Look at that fucking hail. Some are the size of tennis balls."

The pounding on the roof intensified as they looked at each other in awe.

"If they get any bigger, they'll come through the roof."

The children walked in with troubled looks on their faces. "Mom, Dad, what's going on? Will we be okay?" Arianna asked.

"Of course we will," Christina said as she hugged them both.

"I want you guys to stay down here, if that hail comes through the roof there's no saying where it'll end up."

Antonio buried his head in his mother's side.

"Anthony! Stop scaring them," Christina scolded as she led them out of the room.

Anthony glanced back out the window toward Katherine's house. An intense gust hit the trees and he got a glimpse of her front door as he heard a crack come from the roof.

Saturday, 6:45 pm...

Through the darkness Jayden watched the hail pounding on the trees in his backyard, breaking limbs and knocking them to the ground. He thought of the wild animals: squirrels, rabbits, raccoons and the occasional fox or coyote, and how they'd deal with this weather. He assumed they were much more prepared for this type of thing and had their ways to protect themselves. He sat at the table in front of his laptop. The electricity in the air from a fresh storm always stimulated his creative energies and this storm was no different. His mind slipped into a scene he had been stuck on. Romantic scenes had always perplexed him, the emotions being something he found hard to relate to. But now, he was typing away as the flow seemed to come naturally. He finished the scene, reread it, sat back and smiled as the words linked together in just the right order, creating something beautiful; something magical. He walked to the counter and poured a glass of whiskey, saluted the storm and drank.

Saturday, 7:00 pm...

Jasmine slowly advanced through a long open field as thunder, lightning, wind, and hail created a whirlpool of nature, arresting her bravery as she timidly took step after step. She saw three headstones come into focus as she continued her trek. Her curiosity pushed her forward as she approached them and knelt down...

Steven Brennan, 1980-2018

Helen Brennan, 1983-2018

Jacob Brennan, 2010-2018

She fell to the ground in despair as the hail and wind overtook her...

She opened her eyes to the handsome face of Tucker Remington.

"Hi, how do you feel, Jasmine?"

"Tucker? What Happened?"

"I saw you follow your mother out back so I went after you. You fainted. I picked you up and brought you here."

Jasmine quickly looked around the room. She was in a bed in a girl's bedroom.

"Avery's room. I figured you would be more comfortable here."

"Mom, dad, Jacob?"

Tucker looked away, dropping his head. "I'm sorry."

"No, they can't be..."

Tucker sat beside her and held her in his arms as she sobbed.

Saturday, 7:15 pm...

Finally, the hail relented and evolved into snow. The wind kicked up, creating a winter wonderland of dancing snowflakes and growing drifts. Brandon looked out the front window and focused his sight on the Kohler's home. The snow seemed to be falling straight through the front window, creating a drift inside their living room. Elena walked up next to him and followed his gaze.

"Do you think they're okay?" she asked.

"I'm not sure, but I have to get over there to check on them. The hail must've busted through the front window. They must be freezing. The air temperature feels like it's dropped fifty degrees since morning."

"I'll come with you. I don't think you should go alone."

"No, you stay here with Abbey. I'll be fine."

The thermometer outside the back window read twenty-five degrees Fahrenheit so Brandon donned his ski jacket, winter gloves and hat before heading out into the growing bleakness. Instantly, the wind hit him and he fought to keep his footing. He forcefully made his way across the street to the Kohler's front yard, proceeded up the front walk and reached the front door with a coat of fresh fallen snow covering him. He knocked at first but to no avail, so he crawled in through the broken bay window. "Tom, Ann!"

Nothing. He reached in and pulled himself through, being careful not to cut himself on the jagged glass that was left in the frame. Once inside he called out again, louder this time. No response. He hurried towards the kitchen, noticing how cold it was in the house. A faint bark came from above, so he stepped through the vacant kitchen and headed up the stairs to the bedrooms. The Kohler's house was one of the two smallest in the cul-de-sac, containing just a kitchen, living room, two upstairs bedrooms, and one full bathroom. Brandon headed upstairs, turning right down the hallway and into the master bedroom. Ginger sat whimpering between Tom and Ann, who had both lost consciousness from the cold.

"Tom, Ann!" Brandon yelled as he approached the bed. Tom slowly opened his eyes with a confused look on his face as he watched Brandon shake Ann in an attempt to wake her.

"Brandon...?" Tom said.

"Tom, you need to move around to heat your body or hypothermia will set in. We need to get to my house."

"Ann?" Tom said as he sat up and turned to look at his wife.

"I'll carry her, you get Ginger."

As Brandon picked her up he noticed how cold her skin was. Tom picked up Ginger and followed Brandon downstairs.

"Stay right behind me. The wind gusts are brutal; you'll need to fight through them." Tom gave him a nod and the pair exited through the front door. Brandon braced against the cold, putting his back to the wind in an attempt to shield Ann from the wind. He finally reached his front door which had been opened by Elena. He placed Ann down on the couch.

"Throw some blankets on her, we have to get her body temperature up!"

He turned to find Tom, but the old man wasn't there. He rushed back outside and saw him, face down in the street with Ginger whimpering by his side. He hurried out, picked Tom up and carried him inside as Ginger fought through the wind and followed. When they were all inside, Elena batted against the brutal winds, finally shutting the door with a slam.

Saturday 7:20 pm...

The snow, wind, and cold poured through the hole in the roof, creating a winter wonderland in the second-floor hallway causing the drop in temperature inside the house to continue.

Anthony said to his wife and children who huddled together on the living room couch, "We need to find shelter elsewhere. This house is only going to get colder as that hole gets wider."

"Where can we go?" Christina asked.

"We can try Mr. Crane's house."

"Dad, no. That man doesn't even speak to anyone. He's creepy," Arianna said.

"Why don't we try The Remington's?" Cristina offered. "Katherine is very nice. We talk whenever we meet up on the street."

Anthony glanced at his wife. "Too far. Look at it out there...it's a blizzard."

"The Kohler's, then. They're a very friendly couple," Christina replied.

"Okay, fine. Gather whatever you'll need, clothes, snacks, and grab Tiger and Bailey." Moments later they were at the front door ready to go. Anthony held Bailey and Christina held Tiger as they trudged out down the driveway toward the street. Arianna and Antonio braced against the wind as the cold seeped through their clothes and the snow battered their faces. As Anthony turned up the Kohler's driveway, he noticed the missing front window and the elements pouring into the house. He turned and pointed towards Jayden Crane's house. Suddenly, a symphony of howls overtook the whipping wind. Anthony turned to see if he could locate the source of the noise but saw nothing but snow whipping through the air. Then it came again, closer, maybe a hundred feet west, toward Fairview Drive.

"Run!" Anthony screamed as he pointed towards their house. He led the way, holding Bailey to his chest. He swung the door open, dropped Bailey and turned to help his family into the house. Christina was right behind him with Tiger, followed by Arianna. There was no sign of Antonio. Anthony glanced at his wife who had a look of horror on her face. He ran back outside to track down his son. At the end of the driveway, he saw a pack of white wolves, all with red masks around their muzzles, glancing at him in a menacing way, circling their prey they'd already begun to tear apart: Antonio.

Saturday, 7:25 pm...

Jayden knew his neighbors needed help. He saw the hole in their roof through the tops of the trees bordering their properties. He grabbed a couple blankets and headed out the back door, through the tree-line, and into the Romano's backyard to the back door on the deck. He battled the cold, snow, and wind the whole way, and though he'd lived in multiple northern locations, he'd never experienced a storm of this magnitude. He tried the sliding door with no success before knocking loudly as the wind threatened to knock him off his feet. Suddenly the glass door flew open and he rushed in past Christina Romano, hearing it slam behind him.

"We need to get back to my house All of you will freeze in here," Jayden said as he placed one of the blankets around Christina. He glanced at the family, all huddled around the kitchen table with morbid expressions.

"Where's Antonio?"

Anthony just shook his head while feebly mouthing, "Gone."

"What? How?"

From outside came the primal howling of a pack of wolves close by.

"Wolves? How? Here?"

"They got Antonio. The biggest wolves I've ever seen," Anthony said.

"We need to make a run for my house. Those howls came from the front of the house. Follow me through the backyard to my backdoor." Jayden threw the remaining blanket around Arianna and led the family outside. Passing through the tree-line, he noticed a huge, white wolf tracking them, then he howled and sprinted in their direction. Arianna was the first inside, carrying Tiger. Christina followed close behind with Bailey in her arms. Jayden looked for Anthony but he wasn't there. Suddenly, a fury of growls, teeth, and screams came from twenty feet behind him. Through the blitzing snow, he saw red, too much red for any man to survive.

Saturday, 7:30 pm...

The five-mile trek through the Fayetteville back-roads started horribly for Matthew. He slipped on an ice-patch and fell, covering himself in wet snow. The temperature continued to drop as the freezing wetness slowed him down. He left his car behind, assuming the path to get home wouldn't be cleared anytime soon. Luckily, he had a pullover windbreaker in the back seat which he kept there for golf outings that endured inclement weather. At the rate he was traveling he estimated he would arrive home in sixty-ninety minutes. In the distance, he heard howling that sounded like a pack of wolves. He shivered against the cold, pulled his collar up around his neck and continued on his way.

Saturday, 7:45 pm...

Brandon stood next to Abbey as they both looked out the window watching a stray white wolf searching his front yard for food. He was the largest of the group and seemed to be the leader as the others followed him. His pack seemed to be stalking this neighborhood, as if they knew there was prey waiting to be slaughtered. Brandon had a bad feeling in his gut. The reality was they had to make a run for it at some point. The mutant, rogue storm showed no signs of weakening as it continued to progressively intensify. A moan from Tom on the couch broke his thoughts.

Ann passed between the time Brandon entered the Kohler's home and he placed her down on his couch. He tried to revive her, but it was too late, she was gone. Tom faded in and out of consciousness but still alive. Brandon glanced over at him when he shut Ann's eyes forever and saw the pain on the old man's face. Since that recognition of his wife's passing, he was slowly regressing, almost as if he wanted to go be with her. Brandon sensed the old man's decision and sat down next to him.

"Tom, fight this. You can make it. I'll get you to a hospital as soon as possible."

Tom placed his hand on Brandon's shoulder. "You're a good man. Ann always loved you. Reach into my pocket."

Brandon did as he was told and uncovered a set of keys.

"That set is for Bertha. She can make it through this. I added all-wheel drive when we upgraded her a few years back. We always wanted to travel to Alaska. We planned on leaving for a two-month trip next summer." Tom now struggled to get the words out. He paused, swallowed hard, and looked at Brandon. "Take Bertha and get these people out, Brandon. Please take care of Ginger for me. She's a great little dog. I know you can do it. Now I must go; maybe Ann and I will take that Alaskan trip in the afterlife..." Tom dropped his head and closed his eyes. Elena walked over from across the room and placed a hand on Brandon's shoulder.

"Tom... Tom?" Brandon gently shook the old-timer but he knew it was useless. Tom had gone to be with his wife.

David Boiani

Saturday, 8:00 pm...

A gust of wind shook the walls of the house as the temperature continued to fall. Katherine's thoughts turned to Anthony for selfish reasons, and then to Matthew for her children. She wondered how the two men in her life were doing; if they were safe or in harm's way. She watched the snow fall from her back window, weakening in intensity as the air turned colder. A chorus of howls from the street broke her from her trance. She moved to the front of the house and glanced into the road where at least a half-dozen huge, white wolves stood, their steely glances going from house to house. *They're stalking us, hunting us,* she thought, as her eldest son approached from behind.

"Where did they come from?"

She turned from the window and started towards the kitchen. "I have no idea, but they have no plans to leave. How's Jasmine?"

Tucker's face revealed a painful grimace. "In and out of sleep. I gave her the valium, like you said to do."

"Good, that'll relax her. She just lost her whole family, she needs to rest and turn off her mind for a while."

"Mom, what are we going to do?"

"I don't know, Tucker. I've heard nothing over the radio or the scanner. You need to be strong for Jasmine, and your brother and sister. For now, we'll wait here for your father."

"The house is getting colder. Everyone is bundled up, but when will it stop?"

"I can't answer that any more than why it started snowing on a perfect summer day to begin with. We have to be ready for anything."

Saturday, 8:30 pm...

Cristina shrieked and tried to get passed Jayden to save Antonio and Anthony, but he held her tight.

"They're gone. I'm sorry."

Arianna stood in shock watching her mother express the agony of losing her son and husband. She raised her hand to cover her mouth as a wave of vomit escaped through her fingers and a look of shame and horror overtook her pretty features. Jayden pulled Christina into the den, shut the door, and approached Arianna. He noticed her olive complexion had turned white and beads of sweat had appeared on her face. He reached up and placed a hand on her temple.

"It's okay, I'll clean it. You're cold as ice and you need to lay down. Follow me." He led her upstairs into his bedroom where he pulled the covers down and motioned for her to get in. She hesitated a moment before accepting his hospitality. Jayden realized the girl was in shock. He pulled the covers up to her chin and waited for her eyes to close before heading back downstairs to console her mother. When he reached the den, she'd already fallen asleep on the couch.

Saturday, 9:00 pm...

As the intensity of the snow weakened, the wind chilled Matthew to the bone. He estimated the air temperature had dropped to ten or fifteen degrees. He approached the wooded lot that bordered his property to the south-east. He'd cut straight through, being the shortest and hopefully quickest route to his home. Suddenly, a deep, piercing howl stopped him in his tracks. Wolves in Fayetteville, North Carolina? He stood perfectly still and turned his head so he could hear clearly. Another howl, coming from the street. He'd have to stealthily approach from the back and hope something else would garner the beasts' attention. He continued north-east, attempting to acquire enough distance between himself and the source of the howling, then turn straight west, keeping the shelter of his house between the threat. Every step seemed to take an eternity as he walked lightly on the crunchy snow, hoping to stifle any noise. He made his way behind the shed, breaking the tree-line as he paused to make sure he wasn't detected. He started the long walk through the backyard toward the deck to the backdoor and the safety of his home. The howls became louder, seemingly splitting north and south.

They heard me. They're coming from either side of the house, he thought as he broke into a sprint, leaving stealth behind.

He ascended the deck stairs two at a time, and finally reached the glass sliding door leading to the sanctity of his kitchen. He pulled on it but it wouldn't budge. He pounded on the glass as he heard the howls reach the backyard and closing the distance by the second. The door slid open just as the first wolf, the leader, grabbed his ankle in its mouth.

"Oh my God, Matthew! Hurry!" Katherine said. He fell to the ground, his torso inside and his legs outside. He turned and kicked with all his might and connected with the animal's head. His leg broke free and he rolled into the kitchen as Katherine slammed the door shut. Matthew turned to see the wolf stare him down through the glass, his golden eyes studying the treat that had gotten away—for now.

Saturday, 9:20 pm...

The darkness overtook Cedar Court Lane physically and metaphorically. Brandon stared out into the darkness that had once been a beautiful, pleasant neighborhood. He knew he had to attempt an escape and save anyone who remained alive. He placed the Kohler's bodies in his bed and wrapped their arms around one-another, hoping to bring them some comfort. The storm showed no signs of ceasing any more than the reason it came out of nowhere in the middle of a North Carolina summer. The Kohler's RV awaited them. He had to produce a plan to get the survivors there safely and then make an attempt to out-run the storm. How far it spread, how long it intended to stay, he had no clue. He felt a hand on his back and turned to see Abbey smile at him. She used her hands to communicate.

"What are your thoughts?" she asked.

"We make a run for it. Get everyone together and try to get to the RV safely, then head north."

"Washington?" she signed

"You got it. Whatever info or organization there is will be centered there. Six ours, maybe seven in this weather. We may need to find a gas supply on the way but knowing Tom, he probably has it full, which would save us the stop. I'll need to try to round up the neighbors, house by house."

Abbey shook her head and put her arms around him, hugging him tightly. He smiled and hugged back.

"I know, but I'll be careful. We need a plan. Maybe you can help me with that."

Abbey enthusiastically shook her head up and down and kissed Brandon on his cheek.

Saturday, 9:45 pm...

Jayden stepped onto his back patio to monitor the decreasing mercury. His breath came out in puffy clouds of steam that quickly evaporated into the arctic air. There wasn't the slightest movement in the ether; it was clear, cold and silent. He guessed it had entered the single digits and was showing no signs of stabilizing. He glanced around for any sign of the pack of wolves but only noticed the blood trail leading through the snow from the backyard to the driveway. A chill came over his body not just from the frigid air, but the thought of what remained of Anthony's body. With no heat, they needed to move—and soon. He decided he'd wake his guests and devise a plan. He turned and re-entered his home, knowing it may be the last time.

Saturday, 10:00 pm...

There was a deep chunk taken out of Matthew's ankle. Blood had congealed to a jellied, mottled mess around the wound as Katherine cleaned and wrapped it. Matthew glanced up just in time to see his daughter jump down onto the floor and embrace him.

"Daddy, we were so worried about you!" Tucker entered the room and sat next to his sister and father. "How'd you get here? Where's your car?"

He clumsily hugged them both. "Hi sweetheart, I was worried about you guys as well. Hey Tucker, great to see you, son. I left it about five miles from here. I couldn't get through the logjam of deserted vehicles so I hiked the backroads and through the woods. Where the hell did those wolves come from?"

"We have no idea, they just...appeared," Katherine said.

"I have a gun..." Matthew mumbled.

Katherine turned quickly with a look of shock on her face. "What? When did you get a gun? You never told me—"

"Katherine, it was to protect the children if need be. I only have six bullets here. How many wolves are there?"

"At least six, but we don't know if there are more out there."

"How are the neighbors? Any idea who's still here, alive?"

His eyes darted around the room as the faces of his family became grim.

"Jasmine is asleep in the bedroom. Her family is gone."

"No... All of them?"

"Yes."

"How do you know?"

"I saved Jasmine in her backyard. I watched her mother die and saw her father's and Jacob's bodies," Tucker said.

Matthew dropped his head in morbid sorrow. "And the others? Brandon, The Keaton's, Mr. Crane?"

"We don't know, but with no electricity and heat, we're all in danger."

Saturday, 10:30 pm...

"I need to go house to house and round up whoever's still alive. We'll leave at the first sign of morning as soon as the sun rises above the tree-tops. I need you two to create a diversion as I explore the street."

Abbey read Brandon's lips closely as Elena listened intently.

"What kind of diversion did you have in mind?" Elena asked.

"Bait. We create something to control the wolves' attention for a minute at a time, just so I can make it safely from house to house."

Abbey shook her head and signed, "No, Brandon, it's too dangerous."

"I know it is, Abbey, but what choice do we have? We'll all die here if we stay. This is the only way."

Abbey dropped her head and held her hand to her heart as tears fell down her face.

Brandon held them both until her eyes dried.

Saturday, 11:00 pm...

Jayden woke Christina with a wet cloth gently blotting her face. Her eyes opened slowly, focusing on him. Suddenly reality hit her and she jumped up.

"Antonio!"

"Christina, I'm sorry. They're gone."

"Nooooo!"

Jayden held her and rubbed her shoulder as his voice became warm and supportive.

"I'm truly sorry, but you still have a daughter to look out for. I understand how hard this is for you. It's horrible and difficult but you can't give up. We need to fight; for you, Arianna and anyone else left alive.

"I can't...I can't without my child..."

"Yes, you can. You and Arianna will be with them both sooner than you expect if you don't fight. I'm here to help you."

Christina wiped her eyes and sat up, a bit of blood flowing back into her face. Jayden held her tightly.

"We're all part of our existential design, the fusion of our body and soul. Death goes with life, just as a spirit does with a body. We all will live and die. We'll all be together quicker than we expect. Live while you are alive, hold onto every last second, for it is a gift. What gives life meaning? Living it. Living it to the fullest. Never giving up the fight. If we do that, no reckoning with death is required, for the afterlife—the reunion with our loved ones—will be welcomed and that transcendence will be seamless." Jayden smiled gently. "I'm here for you. I'll help you and so will whoever else is alive with us."

Christina looked into his eyes, believing every word Jayden had spoken. "Okay, I can do this."

"Yes, you can. Now let's go take care of your beautiful daughter and figure out a plan."

Sunday, 5:00 am...

The first sign of sunlight slowly appeared on the treetops to the east. Brandon, Elena, and Abbey gathered together all of the food that would attract wolves: hot dogs, lunch meat, raw eggs, vegetables, and even a few cans of Spam which brought some strange looks from Elena.

"Spam, Brandon? Really?"

Brandon smirked and shrugged.

"No matter what, the typical bachelor habits will always rise in the life of a bachelor."

They consolidated the food on the kitchen table and examined the amount and estimated how many portions could be used for bait.

"I think this can be split into three separate sessions. Elena, you can take it into the backyard and throw the first portion over the west fence while Abbey bangs these pots together," Brandon said as he pointed to the metal pans on the counter. "Hopefully, the noise attracts them. I can slip out the front door and make it to the Brennen's while the wolves eat."

"If we only have three portions, how can you make it around to everyone?" Elena asked.

"We need one portion to make it to the RV, so we really only have two to work with unless I can grab more food from another house. But, we know there's nobody in Tom's house and it looks to me like the Romano's have abandon their home," Brandon said as he looked directly across the street, noticing the huge hole in the roof. "That leaves three houses. The Brennen's, the Remington's and Mr. Crane's. Let's give it another hour or so for the sun to fully rise."

They all nodded their heads in agreement and settled in the living room to rest. The calm before the storm.

Sunday, 6:10 am...

Matthew sat on the loveseat looking out the front window to the west as the sun started its lonely journey into the sky. He sat up suddenly, noticing movement on the street. Brandon had stepped out his front door and slowly, carefully, made his way around the trees that separated his lot from Jasmine's house.

"Katherine, come see this!"

His wife walked into the room and stood by him as they watched Brandon continue up the Brennen's driveway and out of sight.

"What the heck is he doing? He's going to get attacked," Katherine said.

"Maybe he doesn't know about the wolves, but I don't see them. That's strange."

"He may come here when he realizes the Brennen's house is empty."

"He has a plan," Matthew said, as a slight smile appeared on his lips.

Sunday, 6:12 am...

The plan had gone without a hitch. Elena and Abbey lured the beasts onto the west side of Brandon's backyard with the food they tossed over the fence. Brandon slipped out unrecognized and now stood at the Brennen's front door, waiting for a response. None came. He glanced down the street for a sign of danger, but the wolves were still feasting. He made his way past the volleyball court to the back deck. He quickly climbed the stairs to the glass sliding door. There, staring at him through the glass with eyes the size of saucers, stood Katherine, Tucker, Avery, Jack, and Jasmine Brennen. The door flew open and Brandon entered, slipping on the blood that had pooled from Matthew's ankle.

"My God, Brandon, are you okay?" Katherine said, reaching down to help him to his feet.

"Thank you," he said as he stood. "I'm fine. Is everybody safe?" He noticed the emotions pour from her as her face dropped into a veil of anguish.

"Jasmine's family, they're all gone."

"Where is she? Is she alive?"

"Yes, she's here with us. Tucker saved her."

"Your family?"

"All here, safe, although Matthew was bitten on his ankle," she said as she pointed to the pool of blood Brandon had already become acquainted with.

"Can he walk?"

"I think so, although I'm not sure how far. He needs stitches, it's a pretty nasty gash."

"I'll take a look at it. Round everyone up in the living room. I have a plan."

Sunday 6:30 am...

Elena stepped out the back door and approached the fence to the west. Every half hour they were to create a diversion with the food, timed with Brandon moving around the street. They had enough food for three sessions, which would hopefully be enough to check every house and return safely to his own. He'd have to pick up whatever he could for one more diversion so they all could make it to the RV safely.

Elena reached over the fence and dropped the pile of food as Abbey banged the pots next to her. The pack of wolves, already trained to the clatter of the metal, came charging from the street, growling and snapping at one another for dominance and first dibs on the food. The pair retreated inside and to the front window to get a glimpse of how Brandon's plan was materializing. They just caught a glimpse of a group of people passing through the playground heading west, probably to Jayden Crane's house. Elena turned and smiled at her daughter as she put her arm around her and kissed her forehead.

Sunday, 6:40 am...

Brandon led the group through the wooded area on the north side of Matthew and Katherine's home, through the playground, and into the backyard of Jayden's house. He had Matthew's gun at the ready, while carrying a bag filled with meat products he had taken from Katherine's refrigerator. He felt confident there now was enough food to keep the wolves busy during an escape attempt. The group gathered around the back door as Brandon knocked loudly. Shortly after, Jayden appeared and swung the door open, a surprised look overtaking him.

"Jayden, are you alone?" Brandon asked as he led the group into Jayden's den.

"No, Christina and Arianna are in the next room."

"Where's Anthony?" Katherine asked, a bit too eagerly. Matthew glanced at his wife as he took a seat to rest his ankle.

Jayden shook his head. "He and the boy didn't make it."

"So, this is everyone who's left. I have Elena and Abbey waiting at my house."

"What about the Kohler's?" Jayden asked.

"Gone, the cold did them in. Their bodies are in my bedroom."

Silence overtook the group. A silence that signified the lives lost and the respect the survivors felt for them. After a few minutes, Brandon took control.

"Okay, this is what we're going to do..."

Sunday, 7:00 am...

Abbey watched her mother throw the last of the food over the fence. This was it. Brandon would be returning with or without any others. She hoped he found some more food to use as bait. As she started outside with the pans, she saw something out of the corner of her eye in the south-east section of the yard. One of the smaller wolves shot out from behind a tree and darted toward Elena. The front paws of the wolf were covered in dirt and were bleeding from digging the frozen ground under the fence. There was a path of blood through the snow from where the wolf had penetrated the fencing. Abbey started banging the pans together as hard as she could trying to scare the beast, but it didn't faze the wolf. It jumped on her mother and tore into her neck. Abbey threw the pans at the wolf then stood in shock, motionless. She watched the only person in her life she truly loved getting ripped apart and eaten by a wild animal. She slumped to the ground in horror as a steady stream of tears fell. By the time she crawled back inside and closed the glass door, her mother was gone.

Sunday, 7:01 am...

Brandon cautiously led the group across the street to his house, keeping the gun fixed on the south-west portion of the yard. It was all clear, so he preceded to his door and ushered the nine survivors and two pets into his home. Moments after he slammed the door closed, the group of carnivores charged through the tree-line and to the front door where their prey resided only seconds prior. Cristina screamed as Jayden and Brandon watched the animals through the window.

"I count seven," Jayden said.

"Me too. We only have six bullets so taking them one at a time won't eliminate them all."

"True, but it'll surely help."

Matthew collapsed on the couch, the blood now flowing freely from his ankle.

"I need to stitch that. I have a kit in the kitchen. Katherine, run upstairs and grab the peroxide under the bathroom sink."

Just then it occurred to Brandon something was off. *Where were Elena and Abbey*? He darted to the back of the house and there, on the floor with hands over her face, was Abbey.

He walked over to her and glanced into the west corner of the backyard. A wolf glared back with blood on his muzzle and a satisfied expression on his face.

At the beast's feet was the bloody, mangled remains of Elena Keaton. Brandon sat next to Abbey and held her.

There were no words to be spoken. Nothing could be said to sooth the pain of watching your mother die, let alone being ripped apart by a wild animal. After minutes of resisting his embrace, Abbey finally let go and accepted his arms and cried on his chest.

Sunday, 9:00 am…

"It's my fault. I let her die instead of helping her," Abbey signed to Brandon.

The two were alone in a spare bedroom upstairs where Brandon had safely kept the two dogs.

"Abbey, it wasn't your fault…let it go. If it's anyone's fault, it's mine. I made both of you vulnerable. I'm sorry."

Simba and Marley each took turns licking away Abbey's tears which brought the slightest inception of a smile on her face.

"As far as I'm concerned, you're now my daughter. Wherever I go from here, I'll take you with me. Elena would've wanted it this way. Simba and Marley are now as much your dogs as mine."

Abbey shook her head and hugged him tightly as Brandon held her to his chest.

"Now, we have to get downstairs and organize our escape with the others. Can you do this?"

Abbey shook her head and followed Brandon with Simba and Marley right behind them.

Sunday, 9:30 am…

Matthew clenched his teeth as Brandon cleaned and stitched his ankle. The only pain reliever available had been a couple of 200 mg ibuprofen, which he had Matthew ingest ten minutes before he began. Matthew relaxed as the pain subsided.

"Thank you, Brandon."

"No problem my friend. Keep the stitches clean and take a few more tablets in a couple hours."

Matthew nodded, and Brandon retreated to the kitchen but froze in his tracks as he noticed the wolf standing on the other side of the glass door staring intently at him. The beast's tongue dangled from its mouth as its eyes searched Brandon's. Blood still covered its muzzle from the recent feast. Brandon reached for Matthew's gun on the counter as the wolf's challenging stare followed his every movement. As he picked up the revolver, the beast seemed to sense the danger as it slowly backed away. Brandon walked to the door, opened it just enough to fit the barrel of the gun through, and took aim. After the echo of the shot faded to silence, there was just the body of a dead wolf with a bullet hole right between its eyes left in its wake.

Sunday 10:00 am…

Everything was ready to go. The remaining survivors lined up at the front door as Brandon walked into the backyard with the food he gathered. He noticed the temperature had continued its spiral as he cautiously approached the south-east corner of the yard, keeping an eye on the hole that the lone wolf had dug. He dropped the food over the fence, circled back to the door, picked up the pans and banged them together which brought a rush of wolves from the street. They immediately found the offering and started their feast. Brandon sensed something was wrong. The largest wolf, the leader, wasn't there. Before Brandon could return to the group to warn them, he heard a chorus of blood-curdling screams from the front of the house.

The Storm

Sunday, 10:01 am...

When Jayden heard the pans banging he led the group out the front door and to the RV. He held the gun alertly, waiting for any sight of wolves. Christina was close behind carrying Tiger, followed by Arianna carrying Bailey, Abbey leading Simba and Marley on leashes, Avery carrying Ginger, Katherine, Jasmine, Jack, Tucker, and Matthew. Suddenly a blur caught Matthew's eye from the west side of the house. The largest of the pack sprinted toward the center of the group. He pounced and landed on Katherine, her throat in his mouth. Simba and Marley pulled Abbey in the direction of the action, wanting to protect their people. Jayden turned but couldn't get a clean shot as the wolf held her body in front of him and dragged her away, leaving a trail of blood. Her body went limp as she weakened from loss of blood. Matthew and Tucker charged the beast, but the commotion brought attention from the rest of the wolves who arrived to support their leader. Jayden took one out, then another. He had three bullets left but four wolves remained. Brandon came running out the front door with a baseball bat, waiving Jayden to get the rest to the safety of the RV. Jayden continued ushering the people toward the RV, but not before taking out another two wolves with three bullets. Now having spent all the ammunition, he turned his attention to helping the others. Christina safely entered followed by Arianna, Jack, Jasmine, and Avery. Abbey was caught in the middle of the street trying to wrestle the two dogs away from the fray. A wolf jumped and landed on Marley. Fangs snarled and growls erupted.

"Oh no you don't!" Brandon yelled coming out of nowhere and landing the bat on the top of the wolves' head. He heard a large yelp as the beast let go of Marley, letting Abbey lead the two canines to safety. Jasmine entered the RV with Tucker and Matthew following close behind, both reeling from the loss of Katherine. Brandon continued to pound the bat on the wolves' head until he was lifeless. Jayden waited at the RV door, calling to Brandon to get in.

Like a stroke of lightening, the leader pounced on Jayden and sent him careening into the RV, his head colliding with the wall then the floor. Blood flowed and pooled underneath him. Christina held a towel to his head as Matthew quickly shut the door. All that remained were the two leaders. The largest wolf, with his strength and fangs, and Brandon with his intelligence and baseball bat. The beast's eyes glared straight into Brandon's, their golden hue sparkling in the early morning sunlight. Brandon could see the wolf's breath flow into the crisp, cold air with every exhale. The air possessed a clean, brisk, invigorating quality, without a gesture of movement. The world was still, motionless, waiting for the showdown to take action.

The animal lunged and Brandon backpedaled, falling back onto the pavement. He thrust the bat forward between his face and the snapping fangs of the beast. Brandon was under an assault of snarls, growls, and violent teeth as he stuck the bat inside the aggressive jaws of the wolf. Brandon weakened as the pure girth and power gradually wore him down. Moments before his surrender, he heard a thud and yelp as the weight and pressure released from his body. Brandon saw Jayden standing over the wolf which had rolled off Brandon and was now regaining its composure. Jayden had a blood-soaked bandage on the side of his head and held a simple broom, waiting for the inevitable attack. Brandon scrambled to his feet and just as the wolf pounced at Jayden, he connected to the back of its head, sending it into another tumble.

Brandon was up and running with Jayden toward the RV. They could hear the beast running after them now, its feet pounding the snow-covered pavement. They heard the muffled growls as it closed the gap to them. They were fifteen feet from RV door as Brandon glanced back, catching a glimpse of the wolf snapping at his heels. Jayden jumped inside, followed by Brandon who leapt for the doorway. He felt a snap on his foot as the wolf grabbed his boot which slipped right off his foot. Brandon jumped up and slammed the door shut, sat down and tried to catch his breath. Next to him sat a battered and exhausted Jayden.

"Thank you," Brandon said as they hugged.

"You're more than welcome. I know you would've done the same for anyone else," Jayden replied with a friendly smile. Both men sat back and enjoyed the calm as the rest of the group silently watched, motionless and stunned.

Sunday, 10:15 am...

After a short rest, Brandon and Jayden organized the group.

"I'll drive. Jayden, I'll need you in shotgun to help me make decisions on our route. We may find many roadways blocked or congested with abandoned cars. Matthew, raise that ankle and rest. Christina, Arianna, Tucker, search the cabinets for any supplies or food you can find. There has to be dogfood on here somewhere that the Kohler's stored for Ginger. If you find some, feed the animals. They must be starving. Place all the human food you can find on the table. We'll have to figure out a plan to portion it."

Brandon sat in the driver's seat then turned to Jayden who sat next to him.

"Damn, I forgot the keys back at my house."

The blank stare for Jayden caused Brandon to burst into laughter.

"Just fucking with ya, partner," he said as the engine turned over and fired up on the first try. "One thing we can't afford to lose is our sense of humor."

"Yeah, well, maybe you should choose better things to fucking joke about," Jayden grumped.

Brandon nodded. "Yeah, maybe you're right."

As the RV started its slow creep down Cedar Court Lane, a lone white wolf stood at the corner, staring into the vehicle with its golden eyes glaring.

"Son of a bitch is looking right at you," Jayden said.

"I see him. We killed his pack. I'm sure he would like to even that score." Brandon waived as they passed and the beast continued his gaze. They pulled north onto Fairview and headed for I-85 North with the snow crunching under the tires and the temperatures now in the single digits. The faint sunlight gave off a vibrant sheen from the freshly fallen snow. Fayetteville had turned into a winter wonderland in the middle of the summer and Brandon was reminded again of his children and sledding on that snow day long ago.

David Boiani

Sunday, 10:30 am...

Brandon pulled the RV into the parking lot of Lucky Strikes Lanes. Through all the tragedy, commotion, and bizarre happenings, Ashley and Steve had never left his thoughts. He had no clue where Steve was when this all went down but he remembered Ashley filling him in on her evenings plans the day before, which now seemed like a lifetime ago.

"I'll just be a minute. Fill the rest in on why we're here for me, please."

"I will and I fully understand. Take your time. If she's in there, find her," Jayden said.

Brandon nodded in appreciation, stepped out of the vehicle and headed for the front door of the bowling alley. The air was frigid and Brandon wondered just how cold it would become.

At least it's far too cold to snow anymore, he thought as he pulled the door open and stepped inside. The place was dark and seemingly empty. Having been here before, Brandon knew there was a bar, kitchen and an office in the back. He searched the bar and kitchen first, cleared all the lanes and finally headed for the bathrooms. He entered the woman's first, but it was vacant and the man's rendered the same result. He proceeded to approach the back of the building and the lone office. This would be his last hope. He inhaled deeply, said a prayer to a god he didn't truly believe in, and pushed the door open. There, sprawled out on the floor and asleep, was his daughter. She had a bloody wrap around her thigh and her breathing seemed labored. Brandon was instantly on the floor next to her.

"Ashley, baby girl, wake up. It's daddy."

She stirred, sat up with a confused look on her face as if she were just pulled out of a long dream. The flash in her eyes was unmistakable. She hugged her father and sobbed as he held her tight.

"What happened?" she asked.

"Why don't you tell me what happened here."

"We were having a great time. Eating, bowling...then this storm moved in. First, it was heavy rain, wind, thunder and lightning. The temperature dropped and it started snowing. We tried to wait it out, but it just got worse. There weren't many people left, so finally we tried to leave and this pack of wolves attacked us. Brian made it to his truck and drove away. He left me, Dad. I ran back to the bowling alley, but one wolf cut me off and bit my leg. I was able to kick him and wrestle free. I came back here but everyone was gone. This office seemed like the safest place."

"Needless to say, there will not be a second date with this Brian," Brandon said with an amused look on his face. Ashley smiled at her father as he tended to her gash in her thigh.

"We have supplies in the RV. I'll clean it and stitch you up there. We have anti-biotics as well."

"RV?"

"Yes, the Kohler's. They're gone." Ashley looked away. She had always been fond of the old couple and visited them frequently when she stayed at her father's place.

Brandon carried his daughter through the bowling alley and out to the RV where he placed her on the bed. He cleaned the wound, loaded her up with painkillers, then stitched the wound and got some antibiotics into her. Ashley fell asleep, warm and safe, having been rescued by the one man who'd always be there to save her. As he passed the rest of the group they all gave him a look of admiration and warmth, for he was, and always will be a hero.

Sunday, 12 noon...

Brandon merged onto I-95 north as other vehicles started to appear on the highway, probably headed for the same destination. As they passed, they'd give a knowing nod and smile, as if to say, "We're all in this together." Brandon didn't know what all of this meant, where the human race was heading in the present or the future, but he knew hope was integral.

He remembered a scene from an old film which he saw one Saturday night he was alone and couldn't sleep. "Get busy living or get busy dying," the old man said as he left his apartment for good to go on a journey where the final outcome was unknown. We strive to live because every second can hold something so beautiful, so enthralling, that to have not experienced it would've been reprehensible. The hope the old man felt in that film long ago now flowed through Brandon's heart and soul. He turned to glance at his people, his new family, as he continued toward their new destination which he believed held some light and hope because once you choose hope, anything is possible.

The End

AFTERWORD

The idea for The Storm came to me while a blizzard afflicted my hometown in southern New England a few years back. As I hunkered down in front of the fireplace with a couple of movies queued up, I imagined a rogue storm that would paralyze society, and with no sign of ending. But this story is as much about the people and how they band together as it is the storm, so I focused on a typical cul-de-sac in any town, U.S.A., and attempted to create characters with complicated, absorbing relationships that would add another level of intrigue to the story.

SESSION 13

I'd be lying if I said I wasn't looking forward to exploring the brain of Ethen Grayson. Discovery is what drives psychiatrists to study their field. Delving into the deep abscesses of the human mind can be exhilarating and even intoxicating to us, even if the circumstances of the case are horrifying.

Such was the case with Ethen.

I'd never met him, but I read up on his case on the internet and always had a morbid curiosity in just how the events affected his mind. We were scheduled to meet today at 2:00 pm and as I plodded my way through my morning appointments, my mind kept returning to Mr. Grayson.

SESSION 1

My first vision of Ethen Grayson as he entered my office wasn't exactly what I'd expected. He was a short slender man, and somehow, I'd mistakenly built his physical appearance up to much larger proportions. He approached my desk, and I stood with my hand extended.

"Hello, Mr. Grayson. Did you have any difficulty finding my office?"

"No, Dr. Pierce. I followed my navigation right to the lot. I've visited this building before, although I can't recall for what."

"Yes, we get that a lot. There were many different businesses in these offices through the years: lawyers, accountants, travel agents...seems like everyone's stepped through these halls at one time or another. So, let me go over the structure of my treatment. I recommend twelve thirty-minute sessions. This first session we'll discuss you, your life, and your expectations of my service. As we move forward, we'll explore your memories and try to discover your emotional scars and work toward healing them."

"Well, that's just it, doctor. I don't have any memories of that whole week. Of course I remember Katie and Ronald, my brother-in-law at the time, but any specifics of how it all happened are gone."

"We'll work toward getting them back. At times it may be very painful, but I believe this is the correct path to take for a full recovery."

I glanced at Ethen to gauge his reaction to my plan. He nodded without any emotion, just agreed in a nonchalant way. I knew then I believed him. He really had no recollection of the horrible events that changed his young daughter's life forever.

"Let's change gears a bit. How's your life today?"

"Fine. I mean I work, eat, and sleep, just like everyone else."

"Have there been any women in your life since...the divorce?"

"No," Ethen replied, and I took note of the loss of eye contact as he answered, as if he were ashamed of his seclusion.

"You're currently working?" I asked with a persuasive shake of the head.

"Yes, I manage an auto parts store."

"You worked in human resources previously, correct?"

"Yes. I was a recruiter for a large internet company. They let me go after the, um...incident."

"Okay Mr. Grayson. I think that's enough for today. Every piece of information you give to me can be of the utmost importance, so thank you for being so open."

"You're welcome. Anything to help."

I walked Ethen to the door feeling that although we'd made some progress with this small chat, there was still so much buried inside, and that I'd have to carefully coax it out of him. I relished the challenge.

SESSION 2

My plan was to focus first on the tragic events which happened to his daughter Katie before bringing up the traumatic experience he himself suffered. I wanted to start slowly, building his trust to a point where he would open up to me naturally. That trust is half the battle for any good psychiatrist. It takes steady time and effort, with an unrelenting belief in the goal. I was committed to this goal, because I was committed to Ethen as a sound, righteous person who just needed help. He entered my office and we started.

"Hi, Ethen. Today I'd like to discuss your ex-wife, Helen."

I studied his face to observe any emotion, but he remained stoic, nodding as if he was fine with that subject.

"Sure, doctor. What would you like to discuss about her?"

I gave him a gentle smile and placed my hands open in front of me in a passive gesture. "Do you still love her?"

"I'll always love her. She mothered my daughter. She gave life to the one thing that matters to me above everything else."

"Am I correct in assuming that she broke it off with you because of what happened that night?"

"Yes. Although, we'd started growing apart before that. I'd have a few drinks at times, and she hated it. She wanted me to swear off liquor, but it wasn't something I couldn't control, so we'd argue about that. She said I was a different person when I had alcohol in me. It was like a snowball rolling down a steep hill, becoming more substantial with every day gone by. I didn't know how to stop the momentum. I wanted to–God knows I did–but I wasn't confident enough to try. Confidence is a strange thing, you know. At times, it's the only difference between a successful, happy person and a miserable failure. I'd lost any conviction and faith in what I could offer her."

"You grew apart because of this?"

"Yes, that and we talked less and less. We didn't communicate enough. We were both to blame and surely, I accept my responsibility in that."

"Did she?"

"I think she blamed me." Ethan shrugged. "Maybe she is right."

I nodded thoughtfully. "How's your relationship now?"

"We don't talk. I have supervised visitations with my daughter once a week and I don't see Helen. They bring Katie to my house and watch as I try to regain her trust and love, hoping to repair our broken relationship. Do you know how hard that is, doctor? To be told how and when I can love my daughter? She was my world. They took her from me; Ronald took her from me." I noticed Ethen start to become agitated and a bit aggressive, so I moved to diffuse the situation immediately.

"You're right, Ethan. That's wrong, and I am sorry. However, we aren't here to place blame, or dwell on history. I want to make your future better for you and Katie. I want you to have a happy, healthy relationship with her for the rest of your life."

He relaxed and nodded his head. "I understand."

"Good. Well, I think we'll end the session here for today. I look forward to seeing you again on Thursday."

Ethen smiled, stood and walked out of my office. I sat still for a bit, digesting the exchange between us. I made a mental note to remember what caused an emotional response in him. That data could prove crucial going forward. I needed a break. I headed to my late lunch and informed my secretary, Judy, I'd be back in an hour.

SESSION 3

The warm sun splashed into my office on a bright spring day as Ethen entered.

"Hello, Ethen, have a seat. Lovely day, isn't it?"

"There's something magical in the air on those first perfect spring days such as this. Like the earth is reborn and all our past faults and imperfections are forgotten. I'd take Katie to the pond and feed the ducks on days like this, before the...episode. She loved animals and they all took a liking to her. Maybe they sensed her innocence."

"I'm sure they did. Animals have a sixth sense about them; some think they can detect evil." I noticed Ethen's eyes flicker at the mention of evil. "Today I'd like to discuss your current job, where you would like to go from here, and talk about your career and what matters most to you."

"Sounds easy enough. I work to pay the bills. I had passion in my past career. I felt I was really helping people and the companies I found for them. It was almost as if I was playing matchmaker...a corporate cupid if you will."

"That must've been fulfilling. Helping both sides by finding the perfect match. How'd they treat you?"

"Very well. Pay was solid, benefits were above average for my position, and they always treated me with respect, which can be very important to an employee. Sometimes all we crave is a little respect."

"You were employed by them for twelve years. How'd you feel when you were told you were being let go?"

Ethan shrugged. "I understood. I had to serve the fifteen months so I had a good idea they'd move on from me. They sat me down and discussed the reasons why, again, they were very respectful. They also said it would be a major PR hit for them if they were to continue my employment when I got out, so it was a business decision as much as anything."

"Sure. So, looking forward, would you like to get back into that field? Human resources—helping people?"

"Not sure. Right now, the passion isn't there. I have anger in my heart and I'm content just peddling auto parts. It's mindless, simple work but it pays the bills while I sort out my life."

"That's just what we'll do, I'm certain of it. My goal is to have you yearn to do all those things you were passionate about before. How does that sound to you?"

"Hey, you're the expert, doc. If you can get me there, I'm all for it."

The session ended and I felt we'd started to make progress. I'd begin to increase the intensity of the discussions soon. The foundation was set and I was confident in a positive outcome.

SESSION 4

The clouds moved in and the sky turned dark and threatening as I awaited Ethen. It was Friday and he was the last appointment of the week. My mind wandered to Saturday night and my date with Robert. I'd started my usual slide into the wall that always appeared around this point in a relationship. The truth was, Robert was a great man and left nothing for a woman to desire, but I still had doubts. Psychiatrists are paid to solve other's mental problems, but that doesn't mean we don't possess a slew of our own. Judy broke me out of my trance.

"Ethen Grayson is here for his 5:30."

"Thank you, Judy. Send him in."

Ethen walked in and sat at his usual spot across from my desk.

"Hello, Ethen. Today I think you should have a seat on the couch. I'll sit in the arm-chair. I want to make you as comfortable as possible."

He stood, walked to the couch and sat in the middle. I proceeded to make my way to the chair. "Now, let's discuss your parents. How's your relationship with your mother?"

Ethen just looked at me as a small grin came over his lips and he let out a quick chuckle. "My mother...you're kidding, right? Isn't that cliché? I mean isn't it a fable that every man's emotional issues stem from their mother? Who am I, Norman Bates?"

I downplayed the sarcasm in his words. "Ethen, it's important that we explore every relationship in your life. Any and all information about your emotions will help me diagnose and treat you in the correct way."

He ran his fingers through his short, dark hair and for the first time I noticed his subtle handsomeness, almost as if I didn't make any effort to notice it before.

"I have a great relationship with my mother. She was a typical mom when I grew up. Fun, but not afraid to discipline me when I needed it. She was involved in everything I did as a child."

"That's great, Ethen. And now?"

"What I did shook her, but she understands. She stands by me and it breaks her heart to see my life turned upside down."

"Does she have a relationship with your ex-wife?"

I noticed Ethen look away in disgust. "Not anymore. They were great friends before the incident. My mother blames Helen for letting Ronald get that close to Katie. But the truth is, she didn't know. None of us did."

"Your father?"

"My father and I don't speak often. We never had a healthy relationship and although I see him at times, we never discuss anything of importance." I looked up as his last sentence surprised me.

"You never discussed what happened with him?"

"Not directly. He just said I did what I had to, and that's about the extent of it."

Thunder roared outside my office window and the ominous sky opened, breaking the momentum of our discussion as we both glanced at the violent rain descending from the sky. By the time we regained our concentration on the discussion, the moment had passed. I wrapped the session up and set up the next appointment for the following week.

SESSION 5

"So, doc, I thought we'd start this session off a bit differently. Tell me a bit about you."

I looked at Ethen as if it were a joke, but his face was blank, steady, and stern.

"Ethen, I'm sure you know that is against doctor-patient protocol."

"I'm sure it is, but this is no normal case and special cases require special procedures. Look, if you want me to totally open up to you, meet me half way. Make me feel a bit more comfortable about who I'm baring my soul to. Makes perfect sense, no?"

I let out a deep sigh. I couldn't argue his reasoning didn't apply and make perfect sense here. "Okay, you win. What would you like to know?"

"Married? I see no ring."

"Never been."

"So, I assume no children?"

"Nope."

"Ah, I get it. You're married to your work. You've always put your studies and your patients above your own personal relationships."

"Sure, something like that."

"Don't you ever feel lonely? Aren't you afraid of waking up old and alone someday?"

I admit this question had occurred to me from time to time, but I always pushed it away. Another issue for another time.

"Sure, we all feel lonely sometimes. Therapists are no different."

"However, missing out on motherhood? I know that can't be easy for any woman, therapist or not."

My eyes darted away from his for a bit and a small smile played on his lips. At this point I realized how intelligent Ethen really was. He achieved his desired goal. He turned the attention from his issues to mine and therefore took control of the relationship, at least temporarily, just to show me he could. I quickly extinguished my obvious weakness and smiled back.

"Well done, Ethen. You should try your hand as a therapist one day after we get you figured out. Now, let's get back to what matters here...you."

"Sure, after you answer one question."

"Go ahead."

"How often do you think about your life passing by without mothering a child?"

I grasped the arms of my chair in my fists and answered, "Not a day goes by that I don't think about what I'm missing. I think about regretting my choices when I grow old, alone and grey, just as you expressed."

He looked at me with what I assumed was sympathy in his eyes, the smirk was gone and all I saw was concern and warmth. I'd look back on this moment as the turning point, the moment he decided to trust me and let me in.

"Thank you, Rachel."

Though I usually prefer to keep my patients at a professional level, I understood what his calling me by my first name meant; he now felt comfortable with me.

"You're welcome. But please, keep it at Doctor Pierce."

"Aye, aye, captain."

The session had flown by and we set up an appointment for the following week.

SESSION 6

I ended my relationship with Robert the past weekend and my mind was swimming as Judy informed me Ethen was present for his appointment. He walked in and quickly took his seat on the couch. I took a seat next to him in my armchair.

"Doctor Pierce, how was your weekend?" I had to admit he was making me a bit paranoid. Did he know something about my breaking it off with Robert or was it just simply coincidence? I wrote it off as the latter.

"Excellent, and yours?"

"Superb, I actually had a date."

I must admit I felt a twinge of jealousy and had no idea where that came from.

"Ethen, that's fabulous! How'd it go and who is the lucky lady?"

"We had a great time, the usual dinner and drinks. I met her at the store I work for. I helped her with some car trouble."

"I think that's wonderful news. Will there be a second date?"

"I believe so, but one step at a time."

"Sure. Well today, I'd like to open up our conversation to anything *you* would like to discuss about yourself, your life, or your family. Anything goes."

It looked like Ethen was turning the question over in his mind, pondering my angle if there was one.

"There's something that's bothering me."

"Go on."

"I keep having these recurring nightmares."

"Tell me about them."

He hesitated, then relaxed a bit, showing another sign he trusted me.

"I've never been afraid of much. I mean horror flicks, the dark, heights...nothing really bothers me too much. However, my nightmares frighten me to the core."

"How long have you been having them?"

"On and off since the incident. Sometimes they cease for a bit, but they always return."

David Boiani

"Okay, tell me about them. Are they varied, or always the same?"

"Always the same. They're always about this dark figure chasing me."

"Dark figure?"

"Yes, I believe it to be Satan."

"Satan?" I looked closely at him. "Why?"

"It's just understood. Almost as if I know it's him going in. Maybe I conjured a vision of him and I know it subconsciously."

"What does he look like?"

"Nothing like the contemporary views of him. He isn't red with sharp horns. He wears a black robe covering his entire body. All I can see is his head."

"Go on..."

"He's human, although a terrifying human. His face and head are black, with no hair. He has these tightly wound horns like they are from a ram, but much smaller and compact to his head. Beady, dark eyes with intense red pupils. Sharp, long teeth with a slithery two-forked tongue, also black. He almost seems serpentine."

"Sounds horrible." I gave him a slight smile to lighten up the mood. "Where does he chase you and does he ever catch you?"

"Never. He just appears wherever I am and starts chasing me. I run and he glides on air toward me, always staying within reasonable distance, but never achieving contact. I always wake up in a cold sweat just before he touches me."

"We all have demons, Ethen. Whatever is cluttering your subconscious is wearing on your mind. Do you think your Satan is a representation of your ex-brother-in-law? What he did was pure evil, so maybe this is your way of dealing with it internally."

"Maybe, I don't know. However, I want them to stop. Do you think you can help me with that, Doc?"

"I can definitely try." I glanced at the clock and noticed our time was up. We said our goodbyes and I went home to mourn my failed relationship with Robert.

SESSION 7

I stayed in all weekend with a few bottles of wine binge-watching streamed series on my new, curved 4D television set. I hadn't put it to much use since I purchased it, so it was nice to feel I was finally getting my money's worth. My mind turned from my clients to Robert and finally, my sister Abigale and her family. She has an impeccable husband and three perfect children. Though my career had advanced very quickly compared to hers, I couldn't help but feel jealous of what I'd sacrificed to obtain that. On Monday I entered the office and checked my schedule. My first session of the week was Ethen and I waited for his arrival by going over my notes in his file. Shortly after, he entered.

"Good morning, Doctor Pierce," he said as he sat on the couch.

"Hello, Ethen, how was your weekend?"

"Uneventful."

"No date with the new girlfriend?"

Ethan smirked. "She's hardly a girlfriend yet, just an acquaintance. I think slow and steady is the way to go for me. Maybe I'll see her this week."

"That's probably a good plan. Today, I want to discuss your prison stay. Is that okay with you?"

"Sure."

"You were originally sentenced to three years, which was bargained down to fifteen months for voluntary manslaughter. I must say that is a light sentence for voluntary."

"I was considered mentally unable to control myself when I strangled Ronald. It was almost reduced to involuntary, but we accepted the deal because, well...I did it. I need to pay for it."

"Well, as I sit here now I can tell you I don't blame you for taking that type of action. It would take a saint not to. However, that's all water under the bridge. Let's discuss how you did in prison."

"Okay."

"Were there any issues? Run-ins with other inmates?"

"No, I kept my head down. Minded my own business."

"How were the guards to you? Any issues?"

"None. Actually, everyone liked me. They backed me on what I did. We all know child molesters are not seen in the best of light in there."

"Of course. How did it feel when you were released?"

"I felt like I did my time. That's it. Not reborn. Not free. I'm not sure I'll ever feel that way again."

"I understand. It's good to feel that you have made things right on your end, that you paid your penance, that's very important in moving forward."

"What I did was wrong, but what he did was evil, which are two very different things."

"I can't disagree with that, Ethen. On that note, I will see you next week."

"Thank you, Doctor Pierce."

As Ethen walked toward the door I called to him. "Oh, and Ethen."

He turned with the doorknob in his hand. "Yes?"

"It's about small steps. You're doing wonderfully."

He smiled and walked out.

SESSION 8

Over the course of the following weekend, I made a pact with myself to live my personal life for me. Stop pressuring myself about relationships and a family and just enjoy myself. I joined a tennis club at the local gym. I signed up for yoga classes. I planned a zip-lining trip with a friend. Heading into the week's session with Ethen, I was more relaxed and content in my life without the constant pressure of starting a family tormenting me.

I stood by the window of my office observing the dark, gun-metal clouds hanging over the day when Ethen arrived. I sent him in, and he sat in his usual spot on the couch.

"How was your weekend, Ethan?"

"We had sex. It just kind of happened. We ended up at my place and she came on to me. I didn't stop it."

I looked at him and I'm sure he picked up on the shocked look on my face which I quickly eliminated. Was he purposely attempting to throw me off balance?

"Oh, okay. Was it what you wanted, or did you just 'do it' for her?"

His eyes darted away and he looked ashamed, as if he was a little boy who disobeyed his mother.

"I'm not sure. It was a physical release, but I felt no connection with her."

"Well, there are worse travesties in the world than enjoying sex just for the physical experience. Don't be so hard on yourself, you can enjoy life every now and again, you know."

"I understand, it's just, I want to feel a connection. I haven't since my wife."

I smiled. "You will, it takes time. Don't think about it and let it come naturally and it will happen. As for today, would it be okay if we discuss your childhood?"

"Sure, it was pretty modest and simple."

"How were you in school?"

"Average student. I was lazy. I passed on my simple God-given intelligence. Never once studied."

"And your parents knew this? "

"Sure. My father was always too busy to get involved in my life. My mother was just happy I passed, although she'd threaten me with punishments if I didn't show more effort."

"Were you ever punished?"

"Yes, but not for my grades. I was always between C-minus and B-plus, just average enough to keep her anger at bay. I was punished for my behavior multiple times."

"Behavior in school?"

"School, home...wherever. I was a little hellion at times, but I settled down as I matured."

"Did you have many friends? Were you involved in activities?"

"Sure, I had a healthy number of friends. Played soccer, loved video games. Really doc, my youth was pretty ordinary. I was your typical underachieving American kid."

"I'm sure you were. I must understand your foundation to better understand you as a man, this is all just part of the process. When and what was your first job?"

"Washing dishes at fifteen in an Italian restaurant."

"First girlfriend?"

"Sixteen. Lost my virginity later that year in the back of an Oldsmobile Cutlass Supreme. Paying for the gas while I drove that boat was a challenge for a sixteen-year-old, but at times the oversized backseat made up for it."

"I'm sure. Any alcohol intake? Drugs?"

"Just the usual. I'd drink occasionally with friends, tried dope a few times. Nothing heavier than that."

Time was up and Ethen left. I had a strange feeling about his childhood, almost as if everything was too nondescript; too ordinary. Was he hiding something from me? I pushed the thought and assumed it was just me being a paranoid therapist. Sometimes we can look into things a bit too deeply. As I got up to leave for lunch I noticed the ominous clouds start to break, promising a brighter afternoon.

SESSION 9

"Today, let's discuss your faith," I said.

"Okay," Ethen agreed.

"Do you believe in God?"

"Now, that's a complicated question. Do you, doctor?"

"I could answer that, but my faith has nothing to do with solving your problems and I don't want to influence your answers in any way."

"Oh, you won't. This is a discussion, is it not? That's what you keep telling me. Are you examining me or having a discussion with me?"

"Okay, I get your point. However, to help you I must examine you." He looked at me with blank eyes, waiting for me to continue. I sighed and gave him what he wanted.

"I was born catholic, raised catholic and consider myself catholic. Still, not a day goes by that I don't question it all. At this point in my life, I'm not sure whether I believe in God or not. I hope He is real, for everyone, but studying the mind as well as understanding the realities of science gives me my doubts."

Ethan nodded and said, "I've been pushed beyond the point of belief of a higher power, however, I choose to accept a creator into my life. I'm not talking about the God peddled out by Catholicism or Christianity, I believe in something stronger than that. A higher power who doesn't care whether you accept him or not. I don't believe miracles happen because of faith; they sometimes happen just because of the rare occasion that the mechanics of the world beat the odds. Most of the time the odds win out affecting us negatively and nobody accepts that as the Lord's work, only when we roll double sevens, stumble over a four-leaf clover, or cut an ace."

"Do you believe in heaven and hell?"

"No."

"An afterlife?"

Ethen paused to ponder this question, his eyes studying the ceiling. "Not heaven, but maybe our souls re-unite, somehow. Another dimension that we can't understand while alive. Maybe part of dying is understanding all of the unanswered questions we ponder during our lives."

"That's an interesting concept. Do you pray, Ethen?"

"I think we all pray in our own way, even if we don't believe. We pray to the universe hoping the odds work in our favor."

"Do you blame your God for what happened to Katie?" For the first time, Ethen looked uncomfortable. "I'm sorry, you don't have to answer that if it bothers you."

"No, it doesn't." Ethen ran his fingers through his hair as small beads of sweat appeared on his chin. "No, Doctor Pierce, I don't blame God. I blame that piece of shit I supposedly killed. He's the reason my life went off the rails—not God."

I wrapped up the session there. It was a productive session and I didn't want to push him too far, too quickly. I knew the upcoming sessions would be challenging for us both.

David Boiani

SESSION 10

Summer had moved in to replace our transient spring. The brilliant sun beat down and the temperature rose into the mid-nineties. Ethen arrived, punctual as usual and we started the session.

"Today I'd like to discuss Ronald. Here, lay down and put this pillow under your head. Take a few deep breaths and exhale slowly. Concentrate on relaxing yourself."

Ethen did as I asked and after a few moments, he said, "Okay, I'm ready."

I sat in my chair with my notepad ready and started.

"How long did you know Ronald?"

"Shortly after I met my wife. We double-dated, went bowling, and had a few drinks together."

"What was your first impression of him?"

"He was much like his sister, pretty straight-forward, no-nonsense but also able to relax and have fun at times."

"Did you always get along with him or were there ever any disagreements?"

"Aside from him being a Red Sox fan and me being a Yankees fan, we got along pretty well. Our political views meshed pretty well. We seemed to desire the same things in life: a family, fulfilling job, good friends, the usual stuff. There really wasn't much for us to bicker about."

"Did Ronald marry?"

"Sure, the same girl he dated when we went out together. They had three children. Great kids."

"Did he ever give you any inkling that he was…different?"

"No, never."

"Did Helen ever mention anything strange about her brother?"

"No."

"If he were alive today, what would you say to him?"

Ethen opened his eyes and brooded for a bit. He then turned to me and said, "I would kill him…again."

I let him sit up and we concluded the session talking about menial subjects: the weather, the Yankees win streak and his job.

SESSION 11

I thought about Ethen that weekend, wondering if I was helping as much as I'd hoped. His therapy was coming to an end and I'd have to make a decision on where to go from here. I knew the next two sessions would be crucial in his development.

Robert called but I didn't answer. He left a voicemail asking how I was and if we could talk. I didn't return the call. On Monday morning I stopped at a coffee shop and grabbed a latte before heading into the office. It was a pleasant day, not too hot, but warm and sunny. Ethen's appointment was my second of the day. When I arrived at the office Judy informed me my first appointment cancelled so I enjoyed my drink and reviewed some case files. Ethen arrived shortly after and Judy sent him in.

"Hi, Doctor Pierce. How was your weekend?"

"Fine, thank you Ethen. And yours?"

"Interesting. Spent Saturday with Stacy."

"Oh, the girlfriend? I'm glad she now has a name," I said with a smirk. "How did it go?"

"As well as can be expected, considering everything."

"You mean everything you've been through?"

"Sure."

"Have you discussed any of it with her?"

"No, I'm not ready to talk to anyone other than you about that."

"Well, you'll know when the time is right. Today may be the most difficult session yet. I'd like to discuss Katie with you."

"Okay, shall I lay down?" he asked with a wink.

"That's probably a good idea."

When we were situated and comfortable, I started.

"Tell me straight form your heart, in your own words, what she means to you."

Ethen closed his eyes. "She was my world; more than my wife, my mother. The love you feel for your child is something totally different— stronger—the bond everlasting. The moment you see your own eyes looking back at you, the moment he or she smiles at you for the first time, is magical; otherworldly. I hope someday you can experience it for yourself, Rachel."

I'd been staring out the window at the sky while listening to him, but when he said my name it snapped my attention back. His eyes were open and met mine. He had this angelic, pleasant smile on his face, and I have to agree, seeing it brought me a degree of comfort.

"Thank you Ethen, that's sweet. However, let's keep the focus on you. Would you say your relationship with Katie was stronger or closer than Helen's?"

"No, they were close. I think a father-daughter relationship is deeper though. There's a certain amount of trust in the strength a girl feels from her father that just isn't present with a mother. Katie counted on me to guide her with that strength."

"Katie was four when the incident happened. She is eight now?"

"Nine."

"Nine, okay. Has your relationship changed?"

"Yes. She seems...timid. Not really afraid, but unsure."

"Of everyone?"

"No, just men. We haven't had the same bond since it happened."

"I'm sorry," I said, and meant it. "Ethen, together we can work on rebuilding that bond. Does she go to counseling?"

"She does."

"Has it helped?"

"I haven't noticed a difference in our relationship. She's pulled within herself. Obviously, seeing her once a week during supervised visitations doesn't help."

"We can work on changing the guidelines, but it all starts here."

"I'd like nothing more than to see her on my own terms, doctor."

I smiled and decided to end the session then. I watched as Ethen walked out of my office and my heart felt for him. We'd become somewhat friends over the course of his therapy, and I cared about him getting his relationship with his daughter back to the way it was before. The ring tone of my cell broke me out of my thoughts. *ROBERT* flashed across my screen and I sent the call to voicemail.

SESSION 12

That weekend I visited my sister for my niece's birthday party. She was turning five and I remembered thinking how innocent and pure she was as she tore into her presents, immune to all the evil that occupies our world. All we know and understand as children is fun, laughter, and adventure. My mind turned to Ethen's Katie and I had to remind myself some children aren't as lucky as the rest. Some learn about evil much quicker than the others.

Ethen walked in and sat on the couch. I was eager to get this session underway, full of optimism as to what we may accomplish together.

"Hi Ethen, let's get started. Lay down and relax." I watched as he did as he was told. "Take a few deep breaths, in and out." I waited a few moments for the breathing to take effect. "I'd like to discuss what happened on September 19th, 2013, between six pm and eight pm."

"But I told you, Doctor Pierce, I don't have any memory of the event. That whole week vanished from my memory."

"Sure, I know you have, but we can discuss what we do know from your police report that night. You were coherent that night. You gave a detailed report, I believe you suffered an acute case of PTSD shortly after causing your own mind to block the terrible happenings of that night."

"Okay, well, I can only relay what the police report states, I have no recollection of it myself."

"Understood."

"Ronald was staying with us for the weekend. When he married, he moved away with his wife so he'd visit us at times on his own. Helen was working late so I'd gone out to pick up some groceries for dinner. I left Ronald to look after Katie while I was out. I realized I forgot my wallet halfway there and when I returned, I found them in her room, her with her clothes removed and him touching her inappropriately. I saw red and immediately went for his throat, choking the life from his lungs. He passed quickly, without much of a fight. As the anger and shock drained from me, I realized what I'd done and called the police. They came and arrested me just as Helen arrived home, that was the whole report."

"And you don't remember any of that?"

"None."

"No bits or pieces in flashbacks? Dreams? In cases of extreme PTSD, time usually causes the memories to return."

"Not for me. Nothing has come back to me. Actually, that whole week is blank in my mind."

At this point, I decided to go in an entirely different direction and invite something into the equation I had never tried before.

"You can sit up now." Ethen opened his eyes and slowly returned to a sitting position. "Have you ever heard of therapeutic hypnosis?"

"Well, I assume it's hypnosis used for psychiatric therapy."

"You assume correctly. I've completed a hypnosis course and I'm licensed to practice it on my patients when I deem it to be helpful. I'd like you to come back for an hour-long, thirteenth session. This may restore your full memory. And though it may be unpleasant at times, I feel it's important for you to make a full recovery."

Ethen paused to take in everything I said. I could see him working through the different possibilities in his mind. In the end, I knew he wanted to fully recover and whatever he had to endure to get to that point was worth it to him.

"Okay, I'll try it."

We set up the hour appointment for the following week and I felt excited and eager to explore Ethen's subconscious.

SESSION 13

I spent the weekend reviewing my notes on hypnosis and preparing myself for the 13th session. Ethen had become the number one priority in my life, and I was obsessed with seeing the therapy through to success. I informed Judy to keep the afternoon free on the day of his appointment so I could further prepare myself. The week seemed to drag but finally, the day arrived. I sent Judy home early as Ethen was my last appointment.

"Now just relax. Put your mind in a peaceful safe place, a place you enjoy and feel calm in: a beach, a hammock on a quiet, lazy afternoon, your warm bed during a stormy winter's night."

Ethen closed his eyes and his breathing slowed. Shortly after, Ethen's pulse was relaxed enough for me to begin my induction technique.

"Relax, you're very sleepy, you're physically exhausted and find it hard to keep your eyes open. Count back from one-hundred to one. Feel your eyes become heavier, you need to rest and sleep. Sleep...sleep..."

I waited for Ethen to pass the light trance and enter the medium phase. Ethen's breathing and heart rate became slow and regular. I saw his arm twitch and his lips move, he was falling into a deeper trance.

"Ethen, can you hear me?"

"Yes." his voice was soft and deliberate.

"How do you feel?"

"Tired...relaxed."

"Okay, good. I want you to go back in time and re-live the occurrences on the nineteenth of September, 2013, between six pm and eight pm. Do you remember that day?"

"I'm home... Katie is in her room."

"Okay, good. What happens next? Are you leaving the house?"

"I walk into her room. She is happy, laughing..."

"Please continue, Ethen."

"I'm drinking a scotch. It's my third of the afternoon."

I'm a bit concerned as we continue. I know Ethen drives to the store for groceries, so I'm wondering if his drinking is more of a problem than he has initially let on.

"I start to undress her, I tell her she needs to change for dinner."

I notice the accounts of this memory is different than what Ethen had told the police in the report.

"Ethen, is Ronald there? Do you go to the store?"

"No, it's just me and Katie, she is so beautiful..."

At this point, I'm terrified of what I am about to hear.

"I reach down, between her legs..."

"Ethen, stop!"

"Ronald walks in on us, he attacks me and strikes me in the jaw. When I recover from the blow, I wrestle him to the floor and put my hands around his throat. He struggles for air as I choke out his last breath."

"Ethen! Wake up now!"

His eyes explode open and he is frantic and furious. He jumps up and puts his hands around my throat—squeezing. I gasp for air and become faint.

"*No! Why did you do this to me!*" he screams. "*Change it back, now!*"

Suddenly his eyes grow large as he realizes what's happening. He lets me go as tears stream down his face. I cower in terror from him as he gets to his feet and runs out of the room. I'd never see Ethen Grayson again.

I never pressed charges. I never even told anyone. Everything he said was under doctor-patient confidentiality. Sure, I could've pressed charges against him for assault, maybe even attempted murder, but why? It was partially my fault. I mean, I did press the issue.

A week later I saw on the news Ethen was found hanging in his house from a self-made noose. I'd be lying if I said I didn't have feelings of guilt pass through my heart. Was it the alcohol? Was it something he couldn't control? Was he abused as a child? I always thought his story of his upbringing just didn't seem real, like it was fabricated. How could I have read the man so incompetently? I've come to accept the fact that many of the questions will never be answered and I'm okay with that.

I've quit the practice. I no longer have the desire to delve into the minds of troubled humans; there's just too much evil present. Evil that can't be explained, not by nature, religion or science. I've started a modest career as a librarian. Sure, it's a long way from being a respected psychiatrist but I enjoy the pure simplicity of the work. I've always been an avid reader and helping others find the books they love is a great honor to me.

Robert and I married and had two children whom I love with everything I have. Maybe what happened with Ethen settled me down just enough to accept the love that was right in front of me. Ethen was correct...there's no other love like what you feel for your children.

I sometimes think about him out of the blue and I can't determine my feelings for him. Anger, sympathy, love, apathy. They all combine to create one huge, confusing ball of emotion. Did I fail him, or did he fail me? One thing is for certain, I do hope that his soul found peace, somehow, and God–*his* God–found it in his heart to forgive him.

The End

David Boiani

AFTERWORD

If you've read my first collection called Dark Musings, you already know I love to include a "twist" in many of my short stories. I embrace the challenge of shocking the reader, while also keeping the twist structurally sound and accessible to the readers who have a bit of intuition and savvy. Add in the cozy intimacy of the sessions and it created an eerie, slippery tale with a climax you may or may not have seen coming.

THE BUTTERFLY EFFECT

T

he giant oak tree towers over the deserted county road with its canopy of branches and leaves shading the blacktop. It was a bright and crisp autumn day with a few white fluffy clouds occasionally bringing shade to the countryside below. A sporadic flurry of breezes cause the long strands of grass on the side of the road to shimmer and the branches of the old oak tree to bend. One solitary, rogue gust causes an acorn to detach from its branch and falls to the middle of the road below. That gust and that lone acorn would cause the lives of three people to be changed forever.

The young raccoon wanders away from his den located in a hollowed-out oak tree. He's the largest and bravest of the kit and those attributes caused him to be the most difficult to keep track of. Mother was down by the stream searching for food, so he ventures out in the other direction to explore. If his mother knew what he was up to, there'd be hell to pay.

He climbs up the steep hill which is covered in shade from a canopy of oak and pine trees. When he finally reaches the top of the hill, he eagerly glances across the horizon and notices something he's never seen before. There was what seemed to be an endless hard, black surface that stretched out in both directions.

He waddles closer to inspect this new discovery. As he reaches the surface, he sticks his paw onto it and feels the rock-hard composition. Unlike the ground around the den and stream, it has absolutely no give to it. Suddenly, something falls from above and lands only a few feet away in the center of the strange surface. He crawls over and curiously picks up the small object.

Wait, he's seen these before! It was an acorn, which mother brought home frequently to eat. He cracks open the hard, outer shell and picks out some of the delicious inner meat, shoving it in his mouth. An intense rumble and vibration shakes the ground. He looks

David Boiani

up just in time to see a huge monster heading straight at his little body. He's frozen in fear and braces for the impact.

Steven Taylor turns onto Rt. 101 in a rush with his mind racing even faster than his sports car. His wife Katie has just gone into labor two weeks early. Steven was away on business, planning to arrive home on the weekend until the panicked phone call came. He has an hour-drive ahead of him on 101, then another thirty minutes west before he would arrive at the hospital. A couple of months ago they were informed the baby, their first, was a girl. Steven's mind wanders to his daughter as he drives down the long and winding country road...

There he stands in the delivery room at the foot of Katie's bed. His daughter cries as the nurse cleans her and then places the baby in his arms. He feels an extraordinary, unfamiliar emotion when he looks at the baby's little face and thinks: Andrea, my daughter.

On this perfect autumn morning, the black Mustang continues down the road as the bright sunshine cascades down on the beautiful countryside. His mind focuses on another time in the future...

It's Andrea's first day of school. Steven parks the car in the lot and escorts his daughter to the front entrance.

"But Daddy, what if I get scared? What if I miss you and Mommy?"

Steven drops down on one knee to look into Andrea's eyes. "Pumpkin, take this and keep it in your pocket. If you become scared, just take it out and look at it for a bit. You'll know we're with you, always. Remember, we both love you very much."

Andrea looks down at a picture of their family, smiles, and puts it in her pocket. Steven watches as his little girl walks away from him and into her own life for the first time. He knows in his heart there will be many more experiences like this in the years ahead.

The wind kicks up as Steven calls his mother.

"Hello?" she answers.

"Hi, Mom. How is she?"

"It's getting close, Steve. Are you on your way?"

"Yes. I'll be there in an hour."

"Please hurry, honey. She's coming quickly."

Steve hangs up and takes the Mustang around a sharp bend. The road straightens, and his thoughts wander once again...

He sits in a large college arena as his daughter's name gets called.

"Congratulations to our valedictorian...Andrea Taylor!"

She's handed her diploma to a standing ovation. Tears trickle down Steven's face. He wipes them away and cheers for his daughter.

Steve presses the gas pedal down further as he tries to make up for lost time. The feeling of anticipation is overwhelming. The wind is blowing through the car, giving him a pure, exhilarating sensation, almost as if nature is cleansing his soul, getting him ready for the next chapter in his life...

He stands with his daughter in front of an altar and a priest. She's the most beautiful woman he has ever seen. He hands her off to a handsome man with a kind face who loves her unconditionally. The bride and groom both say, "I do," and the priest pronounces the couple man and wife. Steven smiles, realizing he gave his own flesh and blood a life that includes love, success, and hope.

Steven is jarred out of his daydream by something in the middle of the road. He jerks the wheel to the right and loses control of the vehicle as the little raccoon runs to safety. The Mustang careens over the side of the road, down a steep hill and directly into a large pine tree.

Steven Taylor dies on impact.

Exactly two hours after her father's death, Andrea Taylor comes into this world in a rush. Just before dusk, the family is informed of the tragedy. Katie is heartbroken. Steven's passing sends her spiraling into a depression which would last for many years and cause a chain of events that would alter the course of Andrea's life forever.

Five years later...

"Andrea, get dressed. I know you're scared, but everyone goes to school. You can't be late the first day of your first year!"

"But Mommy, what if I miss you?" Andrea says as tears fall down her little cheeks.

"You'll get over it. We all do. Now get in the car."

Katie pulls up to the front of the school and drops Andrea off. She doesn't walk her daughter inside; she doesn't talk to her and hand her a picture of their loving family. Katie is still in a deep depression over the loss of her husband. She loves her daughter dearly, but no longer possesses the ability to display her love freely. She'd lost her job and now lives off the life insurance policy Steven had set up for them.

Katie started drinking in moderation at first, but then excessively more over the years, starting the binges earlier and earlier in the day. Andrea spent her first day of school scared and quietly drawn inside herself. She would quickly become an introvert without the confidence required to socialize in a healthy manner. That afternoon, when her mother picks her up, Andrea tells her everything went well, and she enjoyed school. Even at five years old, she knows telling her mother the truth won't help Andrea solve her problems.

Seven years later...

Katie walks into the junior high school and heads for the parent-teacher lounge. Mrs. Jackson, Andrea's teacher, had called for a conference to discuss Andrea's schoolwork and attitude. The two women shake hands and sit down across from each other.

"Nice to see you again, Mrs. Taylor. Glad you could make it."

"Likewise, now what's the issue with my daughter?"

"Andrea is a very bright girl, but she seems withdrawn and despondent. With a bit of effort, she could be a special student. As a teacher, it breaks my heart to see intelligence and talent wasted, and I feel that way about your daughter."

"Has she done something to disrupt your class, Mrs. Jackson?"

"Well, no, but that's the worst part. If she was disruptive, at least I could get through to her...talk to her. Maybe we could work it out. However, she's unapproachable. When I try to push her, she just pulls back further inside herself. I think your daughter suffers from depression."

"Well, Mrs. Jackson, thank you for your diagnosis. I didn't realize teachers doubled as psychiatrists these days."

"Mrs. Taylor, I'm trying to help. I care about your daughter...and you."

"With all due respect, Mrs. Jackson, try losing your husband an hour before you give birth to your child. Try missing him every day. Try feeling the pain of watching your daughter grow up without her father, knowing our perfect family had been destroyed. When you've gone through all that, then come back and see me, and maybe then I'll listen to you."

"Katie, your daughter needs help, before it's too late."

"We're fine," Katie said and stood so suddenly the chair scraped back. "Teach her math, science, history. Do your job and don't worry about what isn't your concern. Good day, Mrs. Jackson."

Mrs. Jackson watches Katie walk out, feeling defeated and helpless, knowing exactly where her intelligent, but wayward, student was heading.

Two years later...

Andrea skips school to hang out with her only friends Paula, Thomas, and Gary. Gary's parents are out of town and he scored some weed, vodka, and cocaine. Gary is on the couch and lights up a joint.

"Andrea, come sit next to me while I set up a line."

Andrea walks over and sits next to Gary. He hands her the blunt. She inhales the smoke then sits back and relaxes.

"Wow, feels great."

"First time?" Paula asks.

"Yeah, never tried coke either."

"Well, now you have," Gary says as he holds up a little mirror containing the line of white powder for her to inhale. She feels the nearly instant jolt of dopamine and collapses back on the couch to the laughter of her friends. Andrea spends the rest of the day in a drug and alcohol-induced high, forgets school and her mother, and wonders what her father was like and whether he would have loved her. She loses her virginity that day to a young man who doesn't care about her or the responsibilities that come with sexual intercourse. Andrea walks into her house at 11:00 that evening to her mother passed out on the sofa with an empty bottle of vodka on her lap, not having once wondered where her fourteen-year-old daughter was.

Two months later...

Andrea says a prayer to no one as she waits for the little stick to share its secret. She doesn't believe in God, so she really has no clue why she'd implore for help from a higher power.

Just another reason to be a disbeliever, she thinks to herself as the pregnancy test reads: POSITIVE.

I'm pregnant, two months shy of my fifteenth birthday. I don't believe this. What am I going to do?

She lies in bed that evening and cries herself to sleep, a horrifying fear running through her.

She bunks school the next day and spends most of it walking around the park, digesting her predicament and how she'll handle it. She'd tell her mother. She had to, because she didn't know how to manage it on her own. She walks in that afternoon and sits beside her mother on the couch. There's an empty bottle of wine on the coffee table next to a half-filled glass.

"Mom, we need to talk."

"Oh, no." Her mother knows as soon as Andrea opened her mouth. "How do you know?"

"Home test."

"What the fuck, Andrea? You're fourteen! Who?"

"My friend, Gary. He doesn't know. No one knows."

"Don't tell anyone. You're going to abort it."

"What if I want it?"

"Andrea, we're not having this discussion. I'll make a few calls and set up an appointment. Don't tell this Gary. We don't need him wanting to keep it and complicating the situation."

Andrea sits there and looks at her mother.

How could she be so cold? How could she just give up on life the way she has? Why didn't her mother love her?

Andrea gets up and without a word, leaves the room and Katie is now alone with her wine.

The following week, Andrea returns home from her appointment. She's sore, exhausted, and heartbroken. She crawls into her bed and lays on her stomach with her face buried in her pillow and cries all night. She craves peaceful sleep, but none come.

Three years later...

Andrea drops out of school. She becomes hooked on cocaine and lands a part-time waitressing job in a low-end restaurant, which doesn't garner nearly enough money to support her addiction. She starts turning tricks for older men who pay her well and soon quits her day job. She hates herself and her life. She's humiliated by who and what she's become and lives just to feed her habit. That sweet, successful woman that Steven Taylor had dreamt about was becoming a forgotten memory. This Andrea was all that remained.

She walks into her house, having made enough that day to cover her needs for the upcoming weekend. She immediately notices her mother. Katie is collapsed on the floor with her hand still grasping a broken glass that had contained vodka, now puddled next to her. On the coffee table are three empty bottles.

Andrea hurries over to her mother's lifeless body.

"Mom, wake up! Mom!" There's no response. Her mother has drunk herself to death.

Andrea sits down on the floor with her head in her hands and weeps. She weeps for her mother, for herself—for everything they have lost in life. When there were no more tears to give, she stands up and heads to the basement.

She knows what she must do.

Three days later...

She is found by a policeman in her room, hanging from the light fixture. Andrea Taylor left the earth four months short of her eighteenth birthday. She died the same day as her mother. A funeral was held for them three days later. Very few people came.

Steven Taylor drives his Mustang down the long, winding country road. He turns to his wife in the passenger seat and smiles. Katie, the only woman he's ever loved, smiles back and grabs his hand. Behind Katie sits five-year-old Andrea, the same age she was on that first day of school, so long ago. She's innocent, beautiful, and is loved dearly by her parents. As the car approaches the spot of the terrible accident that took Stevens life, Andrea notices a small animal on the side of the road.

"Look! Mommy, Daddy, it's a baby raccoon!"

"Wow, look at that sweetie," Katie agrees, amused.

As the family travels happily together on that endless vacant country highway, Steven turns his hand over. "Look what I have for you pumpkin, an acorn, freshly dropped from that tree we just passed."

He hands his daughter the acorn and drives into eternity with his loving family by his side.

The End

AFTERWORD

I'm amazed by the concept brought forth in this story. We never know when a singular moment in our lives will set us on a different path. Our destinies are created by these moments, one by one, all strung together like beads on a string, pushing and pulling us along. Is it a pre-determined destiny, luck, or our own free will and decisions which decide where we end up? Or, just maybe it's a combination of all of these factors.

UNNATURAL SELECTION

They arrived on July 16th, 2021. They didn't communicate with us at all, they just took control. I was a math teacher in that life. I was always good with numbers. My name was Ryan Bradford and I was immensely happy back then. That was the last day of my life, or the life that mattered anyway. I was reviewing the multiplication tables with my favorite student, Courtney, an innocent, blonde seven-year-old, when that brilliant flash of light took over the sky. That last moment I remember was peering into those perfect sky-blue eyes before we were all swept away. She glanced back at me as they rounded the children up and marched them out single file, one by one. She looked at me as tears fell, panic and terror in her eyes as she was quickly taken away. That looked seared into my mind and I still see it in my nightmares today.

The 'Superiors' colonized the whole earth. We don't know where they came from, or why they came here, only that they did and life changed for humans forever. At first, they put us in concentration camps, but shortly after they organized us into different groups. I was placed in what we refer to as the 'slave' group. We clean, cook, build, and do anything the Superiors need us to do. I have a master Superior that I work for. The beings are A-sexual. They reproduce naturally, without sexual contact of any kind. When the time comes, they simply replicate naturally. Their race is extremely intelligent with unrelenting appetites. We understand that to be the reason they came to earth. To feed.

I'm woken early in the morning by my master. Slaves are allowed to sleep but only for a short while. There's much work to be done and if we falter, we'll end up with a fate far worse than the one that was handed down to us. Superiors communicate with us using mental telepathy, but only when they want to. Slaves are the only group they'll talk to and this morning my master orders me to collect the milk from the maternal females. I arrive at the milking parlor and begin to collect the ejaculations of milk from the metal basins. The females look at me as I walk by, their swollen breasts held firmly in metal contraptions that massage the milk from their nipples. The look on each of their faces is pure terror and anguish. They have no life other than to serve the Superiors need for protein. Most of their babies are taken at birth and eaten directly. The healthiest and largest are pulled aside to be nurtured for other fates; some far worse than being eaten. The mothers will be here for as long as their breasts will produce milk, then they'll be slaughtered for their meat. We never speak. If we are caught, we will be killed on the spot. I find it amazing that the desire to live even in this miserable life still outweighs the desire to die.

When I've completed collecting and refrigerating the milk, I head to the slaughterhouse to pick up the meat for the night's feast. Each master has a human butcher who's trained how to efficiently slice up a human carcass for the best cuts of meat. The subjects chosen for the slaughterhouse are the plump and unathletic who serve no other purpose than a meal for the Superiors. Past mothers who having given birth to runts or unhealthy babies and are no longer able to produce milk are also added to the slaughter. I enter the slaughterhouse and my eyes connect with the butcher's, but no words are spoken. He leads me to the day's booty of meat and pause a moment before picking it up. I can hear the screams and cries from the hold located behind the slaughter room. These are fellow humans who know what fate awaits them as they witness others led in to be slaughtered before them. As I haul the load onto my back and turn to go, our eyes connect once again, and I see the horror and emptiness in his eyes. How has this nightmare become our reality? I return to the kitchen and place the meat in the refrigerated box next to the milk. My next chore will be preparing the meal for the evening. I'll be allowed to eat my master's leftovers after I fully clean his dwelling. Human meat doesn't repulse me anymore. I've grown accustomed to eating my fellow man and I don't know if that truth is a matter of me being a survivor, or a coward.

When I've finished cleaning and eating, I'm allowed to retire for the day in my bunk just outside the front door of the dwelling. I'm given one pillow and one blanket on a makeshift cot. I'm grateful for the short time I'm allowed to rest. I close my eyes and I fade away, yearning to dream of a better time.

I awake from my master's thoughts invading my mind. I jump up and instantly understand what he wants. Today is a sporting day for him. We'll be heading to the sporting grounds, a dense forest where prey is released to be hunted. The prey is a healthy, athletic male who's able to run free for ten minutes before a Superior hunts him. The firearm used is very primitive for such an advanced, intellectual race. They use human rifles. My guess is this is to add a bit of challenge to the sport.

Once up, I scramble to collect my master's gun, bullets, and anything else he may need for the hunt. We head on foot to the sporting grounds which are on the land behind my master's dwelling. As I walk, I breathe in the crisp air signifying the start of a beautiful autumn morning. These little pleasures link me to my past and a happier time and keep a small glimmer of hope alive in my heart.

We approach a small cage with a tarp concealing what's inside. My master stands there, awaiting his hunt. The Superiors are slender, with an opaque, white glow to their skin. They wear no clothing as they possess no body parts to cover up. They all stand eight feet tall, with very thin arms and legs. They have immense, oval heads with no hair, just two round massive eyes and modest slits for ears. The lone terrifying feature is their mouths. It's just a horizontal slit with no lips. However, inside are three rows of varying teeth of length and sharpness that resembles the mouth of a shark. I remember being terrified the first time I watched one of them eat. It's as if those teeth don't belong there and were inserted accidentally in an error of the composition of their anatomy. Aside from the teeth, of all the imagined physical appearances humans have created for extraterrestrials, the truth is far more nondescript. They were created for efficiency, and anything not contributing to that had been deleted. Was it intelligent design that fabricated this perfect, systematic blueprint, or evolution? Wherever there is life, whichever universe or under whichever star it lived, I feel that riddle will always be present, confounding our thoughts and invading our dreams.

The cage door is opened, and a naked man bolts out and heads for the cover of the forest. His muscles flex as he runs and I can tell he's a perfect specimen, bred specifically for this day. My master watches him with his large, intense eyes until his quarry is concealed by the flora. He waits five minutes, picks up the riffle and heads after him. The Superiors enjoy an even match; a balanced challenge. Suddenly my master is off, his long legs in full motion. I follow and struggle to keep up with him. I pray the man gets away. I pray to a god who I now know doesn't exist.

I finally catch up to my master as he stands over his fallen prey. There's a single gunshot wound to the back of the human. Superiors never shoot for the head, wanting to keep the trophy intact. It's my job to carry the carcass back through the woods to our dwelling. Luckily, this human was built for speed, not power, so I easily lift his lifeless body in my arms after cleaning the blood from the wound.

We arrive at the end of the forest and my master points to the barn where he'll decapitate his quarry and place it in a glass cube. I then fill the cube with a special solution the Superiors bring with them from their homeland, wherever that may be. It hardens around the head like glass and seals the specimen air-tight, preserving the head forever as a keep-sake. A trophy. My master takes the head, now sealed, and places it on his mantle with all the others. I count five as I pass through the den toward the kitchen where I'll prepare the meat from the rest of the body for dinner. The five sets of eyes glare at me as if I'm a traitor, but what choice do I have? If I don't do as I'm told, I'll end up like them.

After dinner I clean up and eat the leftover potatoes from the human stew I'd cooked earlier. I eat human meat as a last resort when all the other food is exhausted, and my master seems fine with me picking out what I deem edible from his leftovers. My master points to the front porch and I retire to my cot. In the winter months I'm allowed to sleep inside the front hall of the dwelling, but I enjoy the fresh air while the weather is pleasant. I'm not sure how I'm able to continue living this way. The horrors I experience daily have made me numb. I've become immune to the reality of what I witness and take part in. Am I evil...or just trying to survive? And survive for what? Hope? What hope is there? Am I just afraid to die, or am I driven by an instinct to stay alive no matter the cost?

These answerless questions clutter my mind as I drift away, hoping my dreams bring me peace.

I awaken in the middle of the night to the sound of a steady rain falling on the leaves. I struggle to find sleep again and my mind drifts to the earth we all use to know, when we were the dominant species. I understand and admire the sick, twisted irony in what fate has delivered to the human race. We're being treated exactly how we treated animals seven years ago. Have the Superiors been sent here to teach us a lesson? Is there a creator who witnessed what we've done to other living species, species that breathe, bleed, feel, and love as we do? Or, is it just karma, the universe balancing itself out? I reminisce back to my first pet, a golden retriever. I remember thinking how much emotion I felt for her, emotion that was reciprocated. We loved our pets. We'd brag about their intelligence to our friends and let them sleep in the same beds as us. Why, then, were we so cruel to other animals just as intelligent and loving as our pets could be? Cows living miserable lives of production just for our consumption, their babies yanked away from them to live their own miserable lives and be turned into veal steaks. Chickens bred to lay eggs until the day their heads are chopped off and end up on our plates. Elephants slaughtered for their tusks, their carcasses left rotting in the African sun for their own families to see. Baby seals clubbed to death, their vibrant red blood flowing into the ice and snow, just for their pure white pelts. This isn't like how the American Indians treated their prey, with respect and gratitude, careful not to waste one precious part. Sure, I understand Darwinism, evolution, and the way of nature. The strongest survive and move on to reproduce. However, we're humans. We were the most intelligent life form on earth until our friends showed up unannounced and unwelcomed. We should've known better. We should've taken care of our fellow inhabitants, not bring them lives of hopelessness and pain. I finally fade off and I dream of slaughterhouses and suffering.

I awake the next morning to crisp, clear air that seems to arrive directly after a robust rain. The pleasant early morning sunshine trickles through the canopy of a group of trees in the front yard and for a moment, I forget where I am and become lost in the beauty of the late summer morning. Shortly after reality comes crashing back, my master enters my mind and informs me that we'll be visiting one of the breeding grounds shortly. He gives no reason, just informs me to be ready after I prepare breakfast. I dress, serve the piece of shit, and we're off on foot, headed on the two-hour trek north.

We arrive at the breeding barn and enter, accompanied by a Superior in charge. The two become involved in a discussion in their minds. It seems my master would like to trade some human livestock for a few females used for breeding. I wander away a bit and watch as the males are forced to enter the breeding cages behind the females who are chained in position in stalls. If the male cannot perform, he'll be slaughtered immediately and used for meat. Once the female becomes pregnant, she's moved to the pregnancy barns where they'll be forced to lay on their backs for twenty hours a day and be pumped full of nutrients and fluids. The Superiors take no chances that the pregnancies fail from the females abusing their own bodies.

Babies are too valuable.

I watch as sperm is injected into each female but there's no physical enjoyment from the male orgasms, they simply do their job and move on, only to repeat the activity in a few hours. I notice a new female at the southern-most portion of the barn. She's a petite, young blonde girl. I walk over and she turns and glances in my direction as tears fall from her eyes. I feel a sharp dagger in my heart as I recognize Courtney, my favorite student from years ago. This is what breaks me. This, I cannot accept. I run over, free her from her stall, and lead her outside. We head west through a green field filled with wildflowers toward a wooded area. I feel the Superiors chasing us in my mind. There's anger and hatred communicated to me. We enter the woods and I inform her to run north and I'll meet up with her later. My mind creates thoughts of a revolution as I run. We'd rise up and take our earth back, but suddenly I feel a bullet tear into my back. I keep running until another enters my leg and I fall. As I lay on the warm earth, I feel my heart pump my blood into the soil below. I catch a scent of pine, feel a warm, pleasant breeze in my hair and grab a fistful of crisp leaves in my right hand. I pray for Courtney to run to freedom, wherever that may be. I turn my head to the right and my eyes fixate on a small chipmunk looking directly at me. He pauses for a moment then continues on his journey. I watch his little legs carry him away as my eyelids become heavy and I fade away to nothingness and freedom.

David Boiani

AFTERWORD

This story came to me one day while watching a documentary on slaughterhouses. I was appalled by the terror these gentle animals go through. Society makes it easy to turn our heads and not accept responsibility for the brutal lives we force onto these innocent animals. All we see is the processed, marketed, finished product of a burger on a bun or chicken on a plate. This is no more a political discussion as it's a moral one: would you choose to torture or slaughter your pet? I believe most would answer no and the ones who'd answer yes probably shouldn't be free to roam our streets.

23 Cedar Mill Drive

Michael

Conolly had been informed of the fate of 23 Cedar Mill Drive over three months ago. John Simmons, who'd lived there for over ten years, enlightened him with a friendly, courteous phone call. A developer had bought the three-acre lot and planned to construct a dozen condominium units, taking the house and every last tree with it. It was forecasted to be a brilliant, warm, mid-April day and as the sun brightened that early spring morning, Michael pulled onto the highway and headed east toward the house he spent thirty years in.

Over forty years ago, Michael and his fiancé Carol fell in love with the land and chose to build their new house upon it. Located in central Virginia, the landscape was surrounded by rolling hills and featured Red cedar, White pine and Red birch trees in abundance, and even as the region became more populated most of the wooded areas remained intact. People respected and grew to love the foliage of central Virginia. The young couple picked out a lot covering over three-square acres with a perfect spot to build a handsome, stately colonial. Just entering their mid-twenties, this would be their first experience owning a house and building your perfect home from scratch was an exhilarating—although intimidating—feeling. Michael watched and expedited the whole process, from where the house and driveway would go to the rock-wall separating the front and back yards and incorporating the slope of the land into a beautifully constructed yard. The couple weren't only in love with each other, they soon fell in love with their new home.

Michael pulled up in front of his old home. He stepped out of his car, taking his thermos filled with coffee with him and leaned against the passenger door, taking in the house that used to be his home. He also noticing the huge hydraulic excavator that seemed to haunt him from behind a thicket of trees on the west portion of the lot. Not much had changed over the years. The pleasing dove-grey color remained intact as well as the deep grey shingles on the roof. The shutters, however, were no longer pure white but a deep colonial blue and Michael actually liked this color combination more.

The cherry blossom tree on the right corner of the house was in full bloom, exhibiting an explosion of light pink flowers that appeared from the street as a cloud of fluffy cotton candy. He noticed the hydraulic excavator stored on the corner of the lot. Michael took a sip of hot coffee and leaned his head back to absorb the sun's rays as a memory from long ago overtook him...

Michael led his wife up the walk to the front door of their new home. The newlyweds had been married a month prior to the completion of the house and spent the weekend moving their possessions in. Michael picked Carol up and carried her over the threshold to the joy and laughter of his new wife.

"Oh., Michael, you're so romantic. Just think, this is our house! It's so beautiful."

"This is where we'll have a family, Carol. This isn't just our house, it's our home, forever."

He'd carried her upstairs to their new bedroom, placed her on the bed and the couple made love with a renewed passion, which would result in their first child, Joseph, who'd be born exactly Two-hundred and seventy-six days later.

Michael took another sip of coffee and watched as the demolition crew pulled up on the street around him. Two pickup trucks filled with workers arrived, followed by a pair of oversized dump trucks. *Parasites,* he thought, as he watched them all exit their vehicles carrying coffee and donuts. He knew they were just doing their jobs, but that fact didn't numb the pain he felt knowing they would be destroying an emotionally nostalgic element of his life.

The workers gathered on the front steps and walkway drinking their coffee and discussing the hot start by the Nationals. Harper had homered in three-in-a-row and Scherzer was untouchable to start the season. The talk of baseball reminded him of his son, who played the sport straight through high school and college at the University of Virginia. He remembered the night long ago when they took their newborn baby boy home from the hospital...

As Michael carried his son up the walkway and into the house he was overcome with pride and emotion. He always imagined what this moment would feel like when it became reality but nothing could have prepared him for the overwhelming joy that engulfed him with every step. Carol walked by his side with her hand on his back, never taking her eyes off the little miracle they created. Michael placed little Joseph in the crib by their bed. That night neither of them slept a wink.

The morning sun rose as the workers began removing what was left of the windows, doors, light fixtures, tubs, and sinks. Michael presumed they'd liquidate the salvageable parts to maximize the demo companies' profits. When they finished the deconstruction phase, a worker fired up the hydraulic excavator parked in the corner of the yard and approached the west side of the house. Michael closed his eyes and prepared himself for the first strike of the bucket to the roof of his old home. His mind reminisced to a perfect spring day thirty years ago...

There was a feeling of re-birth as the brilliant sun shone down and the birds sang their songs of hope and renewal. The Conolly's were hosting the first cookout of the year and an abundance of friends and family were present. Michael cooked burgers, dogs, sausage, ribs, barbeque chicken and corn on the cob, grilled to perfection, while Carol served mixed drinks, beer, and wine to their guests. They set up a volleyball net and a horseshoe pit. Everyone enjoyed joining in the activities. Joseph, who was now eight, and his little sister Jasmine, now six had a wonderful time meeting new family, friends and interacting with them. It was a perfect day that would be remembered for years to come as the day that magically connected the families and friends from either side forever.

The first thrust of the claw into the roof was the most painful. It brought a morbid reality to Michael that this was real and actually happening before his very eyes. The first strike chewed into his daughter's old bedroom and Michael winced at the sight. The house was extensively more than just shelter for him in the twenty-five years he'd lived there. It was a part of the family, tied to his memories of when his life was enjoyable, wholesome and pure. The destruction of his past home reflected what happened to his life once he moved out.

The sound of the claw re-entering and creating another wound was deafening. The crunching of the wooden beams, plywood, and floorboards was horrific to his ears and for a moment, he questioned his decision to come and bear witness to it. As the violent machine took whatever remained of Jasmine's room, he reminisced about a far more pleasant time, years ago...

I wore a tan suit with a white tie and Jasmine donned a beautiful white dress. It would be our last father/daughter dance, so I wanted it to be memorable for her. We got the pictures out of the way early, ate and danced the night away. I wasn't fond of dancing, but Jasmine loved it and this night was about her. We danced continuously for two hours next to her friends until she decided she'd had enough. We stopped for ice cream before arriving home to top the night off with a movie. We stayed up watching movies in our family room until 3:00 am, but that was okay. It was the weekend, and it turned out to be a night she will always remember that her father wasn't only old and wise, but also young and fun.

A load crack breaks Michael from his memory as the top half of the west side of the house went missing. The excavator took chunk after chunk and deposited them into the dump truck which was quickly filling up. The workers finally noticed the strange man watching the spectacle outside his car by the side of the road. The man standing in the driveway wearing a white hard-hat turned to wave. Michael assumed he was the foreman, as he just watched the workers as they went about their business. Michael gave a modest gesture back, slightly lifting his hand in acknowledgment. *I'll not give you any trouble, but I'm not your friend* he thought as another chunk of his old home went missing.

Lunchtime rolled in and the men gathered around and talked while eating their pre-packed food. Michael opened his lunchbox and placed his humble spread consisting of a peanut butter sandwich and crackers on the hood of his car. As he dug in, he took inventory of the house. The whole top floor was gone and inserted into the dump truck which had departed the site. A worker drove up in the second dump truck, replacing the first. Michael finished off his sandwich, washing it down with some coffee which had turned lukewarm. The workers took their posts as the demolition was set to resume. The perfect, warm sun beat down, splashing the landscape in bright rays. It was a perfect spring day. Mr. White had glanced once more in Michael's direction and started up the driveway toward him.

"Hi, my name is John, John Daniels. I'm the foreman of this production," he said as he offered his hand in a friendly gesture. Michael paused before deciding to take it. The two men shook firmly, lasting a few moments. John finally broke his grip and smiled before he looked back toward the house. "What does it mean to you? I've seen this before in demos. These houses all used to be homes for people, for families. They carry sentimental value and sometimes this type of thing can be very painful."

"My family and I lived here for just over twenty-five years. The best twenty-five years of my life. It does have sentimental meaning to me, Mr. Daniels."

John put his hand on Michael's shoulder for a moment, nodded his head in an understanding gesture, and walked back down the driveway to his post. A painful memory came rushing back to Michael...

Joseph and Jasmine had started their college careers, leaving the couple together in the house for the first time since they built it together so long ago. It was a quiet night and Carol informed him that she had made dinner plans for the evening with her friend and tennis partner, Jackie. As Carol dressed in the bedroom, Michael noticed a notification flash across her cell. It was a text message from Stephen:

I'll be there at 7:00 pm, can't wait to see you.

Michael felt a giant hole bore into his chest. He felt his heart squeeze in on itself and he couldn't breathe. He rushed to the downstairs bathroom and vomited as sweat poured from his face. Why he never confronted Carol about it he didn't know and couldn't understand. He thought maybe he was afraid of actually hearing the words, as if that would verify what he already knew. Although his body remained alive, his heart died that day, never to return.

The demolition continued. The claw dug into the kitchen, living room, and was making its way towards the huge family room and what had always been Michael's favorite room: the library. He reminisced of the great novels he read in the small, cozy room. The walls were all outlined with mahogany bookcases and the only furniture it contained was an oversized mahogany desk with an extremely comfortable office chair and a comfortable loveseat. He'd get lost in that room for hours on end, visiting the many worlds contained in those bookcases. He yearned for those days. He yearned for his family, but the truth was, they were gone long ago. This house was the last link to a different time, a different world, and all that was left was an aging, lonely man who understood every moment in his life worth living had already passed.

Th evil machine knocked the last of the house down and started filling up what space remained in the second dump truck with debris. Michael's thoughts reminisced to a somber day years ago…

The children were grown up and moved on, absorbed by their own lives. Joseph had graduated from the University of Virginia. His professional baseball aspiration fell short, but he started a fabulous career in biological science and was romantically involved with a fellow Cavalier. Jasmine graduated from Virginia Commonwealth University with top honors. She was working in the field as a CAN with aspirations of becoming a family nurse practitioner in the future. She had met a handsome doctor and the couple had plans to marry, move to the West Coast, and start their own family. With the children gone, Michael and Carol had agreed to a divorce. They sold the house and were experiencing their last day together: Michael, Carol, and 23 Cedar Mill Drive.

As the last of the debris was loaded into the truck, a dark gun-metal grey cloud cover overtook the sky. Small raindrops made their appearance and the beautiful, pink flowers on the cherry tree seemed to have wilted since the morning. Michael took his last sip of coffee, but it had turned cold and he spit it out. The workers started to file out now that their job was completed. The dump truck hauled away what remained of Michael's life when he was happy, the last link to a better time. John, the only remaining worker started up the drive toward Michael.

"Here, this is for you, sir," he said as he handed Michael a key. "It's the last remaining key to your old house. I'm sorry, Michael."

Michael looked down at the gold key before tucking it into his pocket.

"Thank you," he said.

John nodded and walked to his truck. Before Michael could turn around he was gone. The rain picked up and Michael knew it was time to leave. He took one last glance at the land he built his dreams upon and drove away.

Michael Conolly died six months later. He was found in his apartment having suffered a massive heart attack. Clinched tightly in his hand were a golden key and a picture of his family. He, Carol, Joseph, and Jasmine, taken at that pleasant cookout in their yard so long ago. Behind the happy, loving family was 23 Cedar Mill Drive, overlooking the people it had grown to love.

The End

David Boiani

AFTERWORD

Our homes hold memories of our lives and loved ones. We're emotionally connected to the houses we've moved on from, each containing recollections of experiences obtained there. This story is about reminiscing those past events and memories. Do they fade away when the last wall is torn down, existing only in some kind of purgatory deep in the abscesses of our minds?

ABSOLUTION

J ohn Collins parked his '77 Oldsmobile Cutlass Supreme and looked out over the beautiful, yet haunting grounds of the Historic Oakwood Cemetery. He turned off the old, trusty 350-cubic inch engine, opened the door and slowly stepped out of the vehicle. His eighty-year-old legs were growing weary and he recently felt his body's age catching up with it. He pushed the heavy door closed and began the long trek to the cemetery's Field of Honor, where thousands of veterans lay in peace in the soil they once fought to protect. The Raleigh, North Carolina sky threatened rain as dark clouds rolled in. John glanced up and cursed mother nature as he continued on his way taking the same route he took every Sunday for the past forty-eight years.

John fought in the Vietnam war, a member of the Fourth Battalion, 503rd Infantry of the 173rd Airborne Brigade, the first U.S. Army ground combat unit to arrive in Vietnam in May of 1965. He spent eight years there. If war is hell, the Vietnam war was where you went when hell kicked you out.

John entered the Field of Honor and continued his usual path to the seventeenth row, ninth headstone, as the rain started to fall. The trek through the Field of Honor brought back many memories of the horrific war. Memories that turned into daily nightmares causing mental and physical disorders. In Vietnam, not only were you fighting the enemy, an enemy who you rarely saw until it was too late, but you were also combating many other unmanageable factors. Soldiers were always wet and cold at night due to the monsoon rains. Adversely, the sun beat down on them during the daytime, dehydrating their bodies to the point of exhaustion. Re-supply was unreliable at best, non-existent at worst, so dry clothes and warm meals were rare. Agent Orange, jungle rot, land mines, and fighting in a country the U.S, soldier knew very little about in such an unorthodox way was truly a horrendous, horrific existence, and that was before your brothers started dropping around you.

John reached the grave and sat down. Some brand new poppies had been placed on the grave and the flowers were ready to burst into full bloom. John glanced at the sky as the rain increased in intensity, but there was never a thought of turning back. This was his duty, and nothing would de-rail his duty. His attention turned to head-stone:

Joe Galliani
Purple Heart
Vietnam War
Not only a great man but a hero
May you rest in peace for eternity

"Hello, my friend, it's been a long week. I can feel my life slipping away and know that it won't be long until I join you. I look forward to meeting up with you in whatever is left for us when we pass. I know a couple of old Irish boys like us are supposed to believe it'll be heaven, but after what we've seen and been through, my faith is all but gone. I received an email from your lovely daughter, Faith, thanking me for what I've done for her and her mother. She's doing so well. She's happily married now with two kids of her own, now adults. She has lived a productive, honest, happy life and for that, I'm grateful. I replied, telling her it was the least I could do for you, and that you were a hero and she should be extremely proud of the father she never met. I think about that often. You going to war and leaving a pregnant girlfriend. We were supposed to be gone for six months...*six months*. Over the years, she talked of the letters and postcards they sent but you never received. I remember you telling me how you assumed Beth met another man who accepted the responsibility of your child and your fear of going home only to find out she had married another. For myself, I had no girlfriend. I had no unborn child."

John looked away in shame as the rain continued to pummel his body. He put his hands over his face in disgust and pain.

"Joe, I'm so sorry. I froze. I should've gone out and pulled you back. I let you die that day. Your daughter grew up without a father and the love of your life without a husband. Beth never married. She never got over you. You were my brother-in-arms, and I failed in a moment of cowardice. I can never forgive myself."

John started coughing and soon spit up rust-colored phlegm. The red had become darker and more prevalent in the last few weeks and John knew it was only a matter of time. He'd accepted his fate and swore off doctors years ago. The truth was, he was ready to die and had been for years. He wanted to accept his fate when he passed. He wanted to end the guilt and face his punishment, whatever that may be. Tears now filled his eyes and rolled off his cheeks.

"I'm so sorry. If I could go back and live those moments again, I would've pulled you to safety instead of watching the bullets riddle your body. As you lay there, awaiting your fate, your eyes connected with mine and I looked away, pretending I didn't see you."

He put his hands over his face and wept outwardly now in great uncontrolled sobs. When he regained his composure, he continued.

"I believe this will be the last time I visit you. It's become extremely challenging to wake up each morning and I know one of these days, I will not. I pray it comes soon. I love you my friend, my brother."

Suddenly, he felt a strange feeling come over him. It was as if the heaviest of weight were lifted off his shoulders and he felt peace. The rain stopped. The sun broke through the clouds and the poppies had opened wide to display a beautiful assortment of colors. All this seemed to happen at once and for the first time in many years, John Collins smiled. He smiled in pure joy because he knew he received forgiveness from his old friend and brother, Joe Galliani; forgiveness from his God, whoever and wherever his God was.

John stood and looked one last time at the old headstone before reaching and putting his hand on it for the first time, then turned and walked away.

Two weeks later, a new grave was dug in that same field. The headstone read:

John Collins
Medal of Honor
John saved twenty-two men,
rushing out into the middle of gunfire
to pull them all to safety
A hero to all who knew him and
To every citizen of our beloved country
May he rest in peace for eternity

The End

AFTERWORD

Absolution was written in respect to all our military, alive and dead. Though far from perfect, they're all heroes, every last one of them. If there's a God, I believe he'd forgive and exonerate them of any misgivings and imperfections our fallen soldiers may have carried with them in life, giving them a peaceful, unmitigated rest.

BROOKE

Brooke

The first time I saw Brooke I couldn't take my eyes off her. I was at the local bookstore combing through the James Michener stock, waiting for one of his titles to grab my attention. She was wearing a light blue sundress which accented her perfect tan. My eyes settled on her long, muscular legs and when I looked up, she had a devious smirk on her face as if she were saying: *I caught you, you dirty boy...but you know what? I like it.* through her eyes. Those green eyes hypnotized me; her glistening skin overwhelmed me, and her thick, raven colored hair staggered me. I noticed her angular curves through the thin material of her dress and felt my groin react accordingly. I quickly looked away to stop the momentum and avoid an uncomfortable situation. As she passed over David Mitchell and Henry Miller, stopping and pulling out Michener's "The Source", I detected her scent of citrusy vanilla combined with her natural, earthy aroma. My senses became intoxicated with her and I temporarily lost my composure, which is a rarity for me.

"Have you read this one?" she asked, a sexy smile playing on her lips.

"Um, which one? The source? Yes, it was interesting." Real smooth you moron, I said to myself.

"What's it about? I've read many of his books. I love historical fiction, but this one seems a bit...ambiguous."

"Um, well, it's about Israel."

"Israel?" She looked at me and I could sense her fishing. "That's it?"

"No, it's much more complicated than that. It re-tells history through artifacts dug up in an archeological site. I highly recommend it," I said, regaining my equilibrium.

"Well, if a cute, obviously intelligent man recommends it, who am I to pass over it."

Yes, I bought it for her, but I also obtained her name and number. Brooke. I'll never forget that name.

* * *

I thought about Brooke that night while I lay restless in bed. It wasn't just a lust-full experience for me, I could've easily conquered that. Brooke seemed to be a perfect combination of intelligence, looks and sex appeal, and that is a combination which is a rarity in today's world. She was still on my mind the next evening when I called her.

"Hello?"

"Hi, Brooke? This is Daniel from the bookstore."

"Hello, Daniel. I started 'The Source' last night."

"That's great, and?"

"So far, so good. I'm intrigued to see where it goes."

"So, I was wondering if you'd like to get together this weekend? Dinner, maybe. Or we could catch some local live music?"

"Music sounds great. I don't eat in front of men on the first date, Daniel. What kind of woman do you think I am?"

"Um, well, the good kind?" Really Daniel, you fucking idiot?

"Men will say anything to get a woman to eat in front of them."

I started to notice something about the chemistry of our relationship at this early stage. She *always* seemed to have me off balance, like I was constantly trying to figure out a hidden meaning behind what she said. Finding a woman that is intelligent enough to toy with your mind is extremely erotic.

"Well, I can assure you I won't expect you to eat with me before you're ready."

"Thank you."

"How does Friday sound? Pick you up at eight?"

"Sure, I'll text you my address. Goodbye, Daniel."

She hung up before I could respond, adding further intrigue and mystery to my growing infatuation.

I received a text message the following day...
78 Sherwood Drive
APT. 1C
DO NOT BE LATE!

I read the text and wondered why she would warn me about being punctual. I just brushed it off and assumed she was a bit OCD.

The week crawled by and when Friday arrived I was full of anticipation and excitement. I left at 7:15 pm, stopped to pick up some flowers on the way and arrived at her place at 7:50 pm. I rang the buzzer for her apartment.

"Hello, Daniel?"

"It's me."

She buzzed me in and I headed to 1C. It was a nice complex, humble but clean and private. I approached her door and reached to knock but it flew open before my knuckles made contact.

"Hi, Brooke, these are for you," I said, handing her the bouquet. She looked at me, took the flowers, glanced down the hallway, and pulled me into her apartment.

"Is everything okay?" I asked as I stumbled into her kitchen.

Her unease instantly turned into charm as a smile appeared. "Of course, let me put these in a vase. They're beautiful. Thank you."

She looked seductive and magnetic in a little black dress which hugged every curve. Her scent overwhelmed me and I could hardly concentrate on speaking. I watched as she picked up her landline phone, listened to the receiver and set it back down. Who has a landline anymore and what the hell is she listening to? I waited while she went through the process a second time.

"Everything okay?" I asked, hoping for a rational explanation, but none came. She picked it up and placed it down a third time which seemed to satisfy her curiosity.

"Okay, let's go," she said, and we were off.

The band began the show as I left Brooke by the stage to grab us a couple of drinks.

"Can I help you?" the bartender asked.

"Sure, I'll have a whiskey on the rocks and a lite beer."

"Whiskey, huh. You're hitting it hard tonight, my friend."

"No, the whiskey is for my date. I'm drinking the beer."

"Um, okay," he said as he walked away to get our drinks.

What kinda chick orders a whiskey? I wondered. My thoughts were interrupted as the lead singer of the band made an announcement.

"By request of Brooke, who'll step in on lead guitar, we'll now play Enter Sandman."

I almost swallowed my tongue as cheers erupted and I glanced onstage to see my date headbanging and ripping out the lead riff. She played flawlessly and when the song was over, I handed her the whiskey with a smile.

"I didn't know you played guitar."

"There's a lot about me you don't know, Daniel." She glanced at my drink. "Lite beer? Dudes shouldn't be infatuated with their mother at your age," she said as she downed her whiskey in two gulps. Infatuated with my mother? What the fuck does that even mean? She then grabbed my beer, shot-gunned it down, went to the bar and returned with two whiskeys.

"Here, no date of mine is drinking lite beer, dude."

At the end of the evening, I drove her home and walked her to her door. The whiskey had definitely sent me into a numb stupor, and I leaned in to give her a kiss on the lips. She turned her cheek to me and I kissed her ear. I tried to turn her face to me so I could have access to her lips, but she wouldn't budge.

"Now, Daniel, be a gentleman and say goodnight. I had a fun time, but you're nowhere near getting between these legs."

I didn't know what to say. I just looked at her as she smiled and entered her apartment, leaving me alone and perplexed. I'd just ended the strangest date I'd ever been on and I was falling head over heels.

I thought about her much of the following week and I was eager to spend some time with her again, so I sent her a text on Wednesday.

Brooke

Hi, Brooke, I'd love to see you this weekend. Does Saturday night work?

Maybe. What did you have in mind?

Festival. Rides, games, music. Then I'll cook dinner for you, if you allow me to watch you eat, that is.

It's possible.

Okay, I'll pick you up at 11 am.

Daniel, don't be late.

As I read her last text, I wondered what she would actually do if I were late? Not answer the door? Tell me to go away? This woman was full of mysteries.

During the rest of the week, I made a promise to myself not to initiate any physical contact. It was obvious she was old-fashioned when it came to sex and I wanted to build this relationship the right way, take my time and be a gentleman. She'd loosen up when she was ready.

I arrived at 10:55 am and waited patiently while she did the same dance with her landline phone until she was satisfied. We arrived at the festival and I purchased the ride pass for the day. I wasn't a huge thrill-seeker, but I've been known to rock a Ferris wheel or two in my younger, crazier days. As soon as we were through the gates she pulled me towards the Colossus Corkscrew Cyclone Coaster, which happened to be the most terrifying coaster in the country. I started to sweat as we passed all the best rides: the little dipper, the swings and the carousel, and ended up in the Colossus line. Having just opened, the line was fairly short. She gave me a weird look as we crawled into our seats and the locking mechanism was secured over our heads.

"Are you going to be okay, Daniel? You look a bit tepid. Your face is white."

My throat cracked as I answered, "Sure, I love this one. I'm just battling a bit of an upset stomach from this morning."

As soon as the words were out of my mouth, the ride started. We crept up a humongous hill before stopping at the top. I closed my eyes and prayed...hard. I don't remember anything after that.

"Aaaaaaaaahhhhhhhhhh!"

After what seemed an endless fall straight to the earth, we went through a corkscrew and a loop-de-loop, finally coming to a stop at the top of a second hill. I opened my eyes and looked out at what seemed to be a miniature, toy theme park below. I saw a freaking seagull fly by. I turned to look at my date and she was staring at me, smiling. Then, we did it all again, backwards.

I got off and threw up in a trash barrel, all while she was laughing at me.

When I regained my composure, we decided to take it easy for the next hour or so to let my stomach settle. We headed for the strip containing the games. We approached the basketball game in which you must shoot an oversized ball through an undersized hoop.

"I can do this, Daniel. I played basketball in high school."

"Okay." I plopped the money down and the attendant placed three balls in front of her.

"Make one, you get a small stuffie. Two, a large. All three, you get ten tokens for any games you want to play today," the gruff-looking attendant said between puffs from a cigar.

"Get the tokens ready, Rocco."

"Rocco? My name ain't Rocco, girly."

"Well, you look like a Rocco."

"Names Diesel."

"Diesel? What the fuck kinda name is that? What are you, a professional wrestler, or did you just step out of the Mad Max movie?"

Diesel just grunted in response to Brooke's verbal assault.

"Well, whatever your name is, get my tokens ready."

"I'll eat my shorts if you make one, never mind all three," Diesel countered.

Brooke turned and winked at me before sinking her first shot.

"As happy as I am to prove you wrong, Rocco, please keep your shorts on."

She proceeded to sink the next two shots as Rocco looked on dumbfounded. She grabbed the token book, smiled at him and we walked away.

I was sticking to my plan of no physical contact and after a while I noticed Brooke glancing at me, as if wondering why I haven't attempted to kiss her yet. Although contact was tempting, I'd continue to keep my distance.

We approached the bumper cars and Brooke pulled me into the terminal.

"We have to do this!" she said as we took our place in line.

We jumped in separate cars as the attendant announced we were starting in thirty seconds and for everyone to buckle in. The cars started up and I was a few cars behind Brooke as she made her first turn. A child who looked to be around ten slammed into her from behind, sending her car into the side wall. He stuck his tongue out at her as he cruised by.

From that moment on Brooke was in pursuit of him. I laid back and watched it all unfold. The punk got tied up in a logjam and she had a direct line to the back of his car. My lovely date floored it and rear-ended him at full speed. His little head whiplashed as his car jerked forward. He turned with horrified eyes to see who assaulted him.

"Yeah that's right you little brat, how'd that taste? Step off you cretin, I own your ass!"

As the ride ended, I could hear the malcontent crying as he exited his car. Brooke continued to taunt him. The boy ran to his guardians, both of the female persuasion. The larger one approached us as we left the attraction.

"Hey, you! Who do you think you are, bullying my boy?"

"If he's really your boy, you should take some time out from crotch munching and teach the little punk some manners."

"What!" The woman reached back to throw a punch but her partner came up from behind and grabbed her arm before it came forward. We walked away, Brooke with her head held high and me once again astounded by her actions.

We were able to get through the remainder of the day without any more vomiting, altercations, or aberrant situations.

We arrived at her apartment and I immediately went to the kitchen to start dinner. I noticed her watching me as I glided by without a touch. I stuck to my plan and I think she was a bit thrown off by it. I'm sure she dealt with overly aggressive men on most of her dates, so it seemed giving her the opposite treatment was an odd experience for her.

She headed to her bedroom as I placed a pan on the stove and prepared to cook a complicated dish of pasta with canned sauce. I turned just as she entered the kitchen, naked as the day she was born.

"You were a very good boy today...too good. I want you to take me now and show me your bad side."

I dropped the box of pasta which spilled out onto the floor in every direction. She laughed and pulled me into the bedroom with the front of my pants standing at attention. Her natural scent was something out of a dream, her skin as soft as velvet, and her mouth tasted like cotton candy. We made love over and over again, pausing only to catch our breath. I must say, my performance surprised even me.

Laying side by side after the final session my stomach issues resurfaced and I accidentally let out some silent gas. She immediately looked up at me and said, "Dude, that's weak. If you're going to do it, let it rip." She proceeded to lift her leg and blow the loudest fart I'd ever heard, which, amazingly enough, smelled of cotton candy.

"Daniel, you do realize our souls are connected now. I believe souls have a mind of their own and they spend our lives seeking out a soul-mate. We're now connected, like yin and yang, until death do we part."

I must admit, for the first time I felt nervous about Brooke. Even after all the antics I never got the feeling she was a bit...off. Little did I realize at the time how wrong I was, and how quickly things would get darker.

Brooke

* * *

I called my lifelong friend Andrew the following day just to gain some perspective. He answered on the first ring.

"Hey dude, what's it been, three weeks? How's everything?"

"I need your help, man."

"Shoot."

"You ever date a woman who frightened you?"

"Frightened? In what way?"

"Just kinda made you feel...odd."

"Sure, I guess. Break up with her."

"Well, that's just it. She's incredible. Intelligent, gorgeous, but also down to earth. She's like dating a dude you're sexually attracted to. I mean, a dude that's a woman. You know what I mean."

"Okay then stop looking for issues and enjoy it. If you have fun with her, what's the problem?"

"Something is just off."

"Dude, smoke a bone and relax. Don't be so fucking uptight. Let's double date sometime and I'll give you my opinion, but I'm sure it's just in your head."

"You're probably right. Let me set something up. I'll be in touch."

"Peace out."

We hung up and our conversation eased my mind, until Brooke called me the following day.

I was at work in between appointments when she called.

"Hi, what's up?"

"Oh, Daniel, you'll never guess who I'm having lunch with."

"Um, you're right, I don't know."

"Your mom!"

"What?"

"Yeah, I called her up and told her we're practically engaged and would love to meet the mother of my true love."

"Brooke, where the hell did you get her number?"

"I tracked it through your social media accounts. Found her profile and name, the rest was easy. We're going to take a yoga class together."

"What? Are you serious? Brooke, you searched out my mom without telling me?"

"Oh, don't be upset, lover boy. This'll bring us closer together. She says hi!"

I didn't know what else to say. I called my Mom later that evening to make sure her story was accurate and my mother confirmed it. On top of that, she said she loved Brooke and I finally had picked out a decent girlfriend. I hung up and stared at the ceiling until I fell asleep a few hours later.

We met Andrew and his longtime girlfriend, Jamie the following Saturday night for drinks. I noticed Andrew looking Brooke up and down when we walked in. Jamie was a cute girl, but she was no match for the sexiness that Brooke exuded, dressed in tight jeans and white halter top. As Brooke noticed my friend's glances, she monitored me to see if I had a reaction to his lust-filled stare, but I played it off like I didn't notice. Andrew had been with Jamie so long and they were so secure in their relationship that they were both fine with the occasional stray, lust-driven glance at another.

We walked up to the bar and I greeted my friends.

"Andrew, Jamie, this is Brooke."

"Hello, Brooke," Jamie said.

"Brooke, Daniel informed me of your beauty and I must say, he didn't exaggerate," Andrew said.

"Thank you, Andrew." She turned to Jamie and said, "I'm shocked you would notice another's beauty when you have such an enchanting, desirable woman on your arm."

Jamie grinned at that. "Thank you, Brooke, sometimes men don't realize what they have in front of them. The grass is always greener and all that."

"Very true and I'm sure Daniel knows exactly what he has. So, how did you all meet?"

"I actually met Andrew through Jamie in school a long time ago. They've been together since."

"Oh, that's a wonderful story. My little matchmaker," Brooke said with an odd tone in her voice.

I moved to change the subject. "So, let's get a table and play some pool."

When seated, Andrew and I sauntered over to the bar to grab a round of drinks. I looked back and Brooke was racking the balls and picking out a cue stick. Don't tell me she's a pro at billiards as well, I thought.

"So, what do you think?" I gave Andrew my best *don't bullshit me* look.

"Dude, she's fucking hot."

"Yeah, I know that. But do you get any odd vibes from her?"

"No, not yet."

"Well, pay attention to her."

Andrew smiled as if to say he would enjoy helping me out on keeping an eye on her.

I, of course, ordered two whiskey's while Andrew ordered a couple of beers and we headed back to the ladies.

We played pool, mixing up partners each game and Brooke acted perfectly normal. The craziness from our other two dates together was entirely gone and all that was left was this perfect, lovely lady, enjoying an evening out with her man and a few of his friends. Andrew told me to stop being paranoid and Brooke and Jamie actually exchanged numbers. They agreed to meet for drinks sometime–a ladies' night out–as they put it. Everything was perfect, until we left my friends and headed home alone.

"Did you fuck her?"

"What? No..."

"Daniel, do *not* bullshit me. I can tell sexual angst when I see it. She wanted your cock. Did you fuck her?"

"Brooke, never. We were just friends."

"Sure, cause all men and women can just be...friends."

As I drove on, ignoring her craziness, she placed her hand on my crotch and started undoing my pants.

"Brooke, what…"

"Shhhh, you know you want it; let me play."

I swallowed hard as she freed my penis from its prison and started stroking it. Suddenly her grasp tightened, and I felt pain as her nails dug into my sacred flesh.

"*Did you fuck her?*

"Brooke, what are you doing? That hurts! No, I never screwed her, honestly. Pleases let go."

"I believe you—now."

She then bowed her head in my lap and performed oral sex on me while I drove. I was doing twenty MPH on the highway and multiple vehicles drove by, angrily honking their horns. I had to pull over because I almost hit fourteen cars while she implemented her talents on me. Yes, fourteen. I counted. She finished on the side of a busy road with people walking by and headlights passing on our left. Even with all the distraction, it was the best orgasm I ever had in my life. It took me fifteen minutes to regain my composure enough to drive us home. She laughed all the way.

For the following weeks, her favorite activity was performing oral sex on me, although it seemed she had a negative reaction to the taste, or so I thought at the time. When I would ejaculate in her mouth she would rush into the bathroom to spit it out. One night as she rushed to spit, my mind traveled back to the evening in my car when she did it for the first time and swallowed it without an issue. Something in my mind clicked and I asked her about it when she returned to bed.

"Daniel, I've always spit. I hope that doesn't bother you."

"I really don't care either way, I just thought it weird that you'd suddenly change."

"It's in your mind. Go to sleep."

I stared at the ceiling as she dozed off. My mind kept returning to the night and my certainty of the event. I got up to relieve myself and decided to do a bit of detective work. I mean, how closely did I really know the woman I was currently sharing a bed with? I checked her medicine cabinet which revealed an army of anti-depressants. That didn't startle me, I knew the number of people in the world today taking anti-depressants was staggering; the fact she had so many different ones is what disturbed me. Did she mix them? Did she keep trying different types because none of them worked? What the fuck was she like without them?

I left the bathroom and headed to the kitchen for a cold drink of water. There were no bottles in the fridge, so I poured a glass from the tap. I opened the freezer to add a few ice-cubes and what I saw froze me in horror. Five small test-tubes filed with a white substance.

I couldn't move. My whole life flashed before me. I felt like I was outside my body viewing my own horror reality show. I reached down, picked one up, and turned it over in my hand. My worst nightmare was turning real. A small label covered the backside of the tube with the word *Daniel: semen* typed neatly in tiny letters. My mind raced. What did this mean? Was she spitting my freshly spewed sperm into a test-tube each time she blew me? Was she secretly trying to become pregnant with my sperm? I always used condoms and she claimed she was on the pill. Thinking back, she would ask me to put the condoms aside and make true, real, flesh to flesh love, which I never did. Was she just trying to trick me? Was this an elaborate plan to mother my child without my consent?

A shiver went up my spine and I quickly rounded up my semen samples and threw them into the microwave. I cooked those little bastards for a minute each to make sure they wouldn't sabotage me. To think, my own semen was part of this dishonest scheme, I wasn't sure if I could trust my own body anymore.

After cooking my boys, I crawled back into bed thinking about how I should handle this with her. She obviously struggled with reality and for the first time, I worried about how dangerous being involved with her in this way could be. In the end, I decided talking to her about it would solve nothing. I knew what she was planning on doing with my sperm just as she did, so why even bring it up? You can't discuss reason with someone who isn't in touch with reality. I tried to close my eyes and sleep. None came.

Aside from a few texts, I avoided her the following week. She left a few voicemails wondering what I was doing, if something was wrong, and when would she'd see me again. I never brought up the saved semen. I mean, how do you start that conversation? *Honey, I saw what you have stored in your freezer.* Or, *Baby, why are you saving my sperm?* Even more lame, *Sweetheart, what's up with my semen in your ice-box?* The truth is, it freaked me the fuck out and the less I thought about it the better. She sent me a text on Thursday night.

Hello Daniel, can I stop by and say hi?

I stared at my phone deciding how to respond.

I'm actually out right now. Maybe we can hook up this weekend.

That's strange, cause I'm sitting in your driveway you fucking liar. Why, Daniel? Why are you lying to me?

I glanced out the window and there was her car, behind mine.

I'm sorry, Brooke, I just don't feel that well today.

Well, why the fuck didn't you say that? I'll come in and take care of you.

I'd rather just crash and go—

In the middle of typing my text, the front door opened and she walked in.

"How did you...?"

"I made an extra set of your keys one weekend when you were over. Remember when you were asleep on my couch, and I went to pick up take out for us?"

"But, why...?

"Now, baby, come with me. I'll put you to bed and take care of you."

At this point, I was confused and fearful of what she would do or say next, so I did as she asked. I had also just worked two long shifts back-to-back, so I was exhausted and needed the sleep. She made me chicken soup that I ate before crawling in bed. I woke with her next to me, both of us naked. I don't remember anything after the soup. Did she drug me?

"What time is it?" I asked.

"Go back to sleep sweetie. It's 10 AM."

I jumped up. "Ten in the morning? I have to get to work."

"No silly, I called in for you."

"How? Where did you get the number?"

"Your phone, of course. I know your passcode. You really shouldn't use your birthdate...it's so obvious."

I grabbed my phone and headed to the bathroom. She lay back with a sinister smile on her face. I shut the door and sat on the toilet and quickly searched my phone for anything else she may have seen. The photos of all my ex-girlfriends were gone as well as every number represented by a female name. She replaced my wallpaper and screen saver images with pictures of her. I dropped my phone and put my hands over my face.

When I came out, I quickly got dressed.

"I need to get to work," I said quickly. "There's something I need to get done today. I'll call you later."

She stared at me, pondering if I meant what I said or if I was just trying to get rid of her. Finally, she got up, dressed and walked out with me. She kissed me and drove away. I instantly called a locksmith to change my locks. I realized at this point the relationship had to end.

I avoided Brooke the following week. She sent texts, left voicemails, and even emailed me, but I failed to respond to any of her attempts to connect. Just when I thought I may pull off a clean break, I received a text message attached to a picture on Saturday.

Hi Daniel, we're out eating lunch together. We may even head to the mall for some shopping. Would love to see you tonight, after I drop your mother off safely, that is.

The picture was of her and my mother with their arms around each other, both wearing wide, happy smiles. I finally saw it. The crazy in her eyes. The lunacy in her smile. I never was able to detect it before but in that picture on that Saturday afternoon, it was as evident as the sunshine pouring down all around them. I started to panic. I picked up on the subtle message in her text. "After I drop your mother off safely, that is…" If I didn't agree with meeting her, my mother may be in danger. I responded…

Okay, drop her off and come to my house.

She texted back a smiley face and a big red heart. I just about threw up in my mouth.

She arrived a few hours later and unsuccessfully tried using her duplicate key on my door. My phone rang shortly after.

"HI, I'll be right out."

"Why, Daniel? Why would you lock me out?"

I hung up on her and headed outside.

She looked up at me as I pulled my front door shut behind me. I noticed her eyes were wet. She had started to cry. She approached me and put her arms around me.

"Why, Daniel?"

"You scared me. Your behavior has been…unusual, to say the least."

"Daniel, I love you. I would do anything for you." She started to shout and become unhinged. Why I said what I did next, I'll never know. I think it's that men seem to think they can handle any situation placed in front of them, that they're invincible. I fell into the same trap and I couldn't have been more wrong.

"I don't want to talk about this here, let's do for a ride," I said.

We got in her car and she drove us away from my house.

"Want to go to my place? You can spend the night."

"I don't think that's a good idea, Brooke."

I felt her glance over at me as she drove onto the highway.

"Look what I did for you, Daniel."

She held her forearm up so I could see my initials, D.M., carved into her flesh.

I freaked.

"*Are you fucking insane?* Why would you do that? We had good sex and fun times, but we obviously can't be together. You need help, Brooke. You have issues."

"We all have issues, Daniel. I embrace mine, you run from yours." I noticed the speed of the vehicle pick up as the intensity of the discussion rose. I reached over and buckled my seatbelt.

"What the fuck does that mean? What issues do I have?"

"You can't connect with your true feelings. Yeah, I'm nuts at times, but I know true love when I feel it. You fight it because it's easier that way."

"You threatened to hurt my mother if I didn't see you tonight. You call that love?"

"I would never hurt your mother. We're great friends and have so much in common."

"Oh, really?"

"We both love you, dearly, Daniel. I told her myself today. She misses you, Daniel. You hardly spend any time with her."

"Please slow down. You're going to kill us."

She looked over at me, smiled, and pressed the accelerator to the floor. The next thirty seconds were a blur. She turned off the highway and steered toward a tree on the bank. The last thing I remember is screaming and the sound of twisted metal...

I slowly opened my eyes. I was in a hospital bed a full day later. My mother was by my bedside and I moved to sit up.

"Mom, what...?"

"Daniel! Don't move honey, just rest. I'll get the nurse."

"Mom, Brooke...?"

She looked at me with a sad face and just shook her head. She was gone, off the earth and out of my life. I shut my eyes and drifted off.

I was fine. I had a bump on my head and a few bruises, but no injuries that wouldn't heal in a short amount of time. Brooke was another story. She never buckled her seatbelt. Her body was ejected from the vehicle on contact and she died instantly.

I walked into the funeral home to an empty room with a closed casket. She had no family, no friends. She was truly alone in life and I felt a wave of guilt as I bowed my head to say a prayer. My mother walked up beside me.

"You know, Daniel, she really cared about you."

"Mom, she was crazy."

"She had issues, baby, but she had a good heart. We really connected and she opened up to me. She was molested as a child by her father. Her mother did nothing, just let it happen. She disowned them both. She found it hard to trust people, but she told me you were different. She said your connection was real. She just wished she could control her demons; her insecurities."

I turned to look at her. "Do you even know what she did? The crazy antics?"

"Did she ever hurt you?"

"Other than attempting to kill me in her car?"

"I can't forgive her for that, but I can understand. She wanted to spend eternity with you."

"Mom, she told me something about you, about us."

She turned away, afraid to talk to me about it.

"Do you really feel that I don't make an attempt to see you?"

"Yes, if I don't make the attempt, we'd never talk or see each other. I'm growing older, Daniel. I want to spend as much time as I can with you before I die. Life goes by in a flash. You'll understand at some point."

I reached over and hugged her. Tears fell as I held her tight.

Years later, I find myself thanking Brooke for bringing us closer together. My mother and I are now best friends and I'm proud to say I'm married with two children she adores.

I think about Brooke often. At times I miss her, other times I remember her as an unstable lunatic. But when I think back to our relationship, my mother was right...she never hurt me. She always tried to help me, comfort me. Maybe she loved me too much, if that's possible. Either way, I hope she has found peace with herself and God.

R.I.P. Brooke...

The End

David Boiani

AFTERWORD

This tale was born while hearing the horror stories of my friends dating escapades. If you've read Dark Musings, you know of a little story called 'Aaron.' Brooke is a loose reflection on Aaron, only from a male's perspective.

SIX DEGREES

Amber, 7 am...

Amber woke to Riley stumbling into the bathroom and missing the toilet with an endless stream of urine. She put her hand to her head and wondered why she pushed him to stand for the last two months. She pulled the covers back and hurried into the bathroom, pausing to grab the disinfectant and a towel.

"Mommy, Mommy, I did it! I turned the water yellow, come thee!"

She never tired of Riley's lisp and although she knew speech therapists in school would all but extinguish it, she'd enjoy it while it lasted.

"Oh, baby, good job. However, you've seemed to miss a bit. See? You want to get it all in the bowl to make the water as yellow as can be."

"Okay, Mommy. I thorry."

Hearing the lisp and Riley's humble innocence melted her heart. He was the reason she did it. The reason she chose this lifestyle. One day she may look back and regret it, but for now she had to continue for Riley's sake. Shelter, food, and clothing didn't pay for themselves, and that doesn't even include medical bills which were more prominent with Riley than the average child. His asthma needed constant attention as his labored breathing quickly transformed into coughing fits, wheezing, and even chest pain at times.

"It's okay, honey, just keep working at it. Practice makes perfect. Now, go back to bed. You need more rest."

She tucked her boy back in and returned to her bed and called Peter, one of her clients.

"Hi, Peter, I have you down for seven tonight. Three hours."

"Hi Am, yes, can't wait."

"See you then."

She ended the call placed her phone aside. Tears came as they usually did when she was alone with nothing but her thoughts and regrets. She wished there was a better way.

Two hours later she dropped Riley off at pre-school and headed to her favorite coffee shop to start her working day. She had a ten am, twelve pm, one pm and finally Peter at seven. She walked up to the counter and ordered her black French Roast.

Tracy, 9 am...

The morning crowd buzzed as the shop filled with customers craving their morning fix of joe. A pretty blonde stepped up to the counter and a sting of jealousy came over Tracy. Why couldn't she have glorious blonde hair, a welcoming smile, and pretty, blue eyes?

"Hi, may I help you?"

"Yes, French Roast...black, please."

"Sure, coming right up. Your name?"

"Amber."

Tracy poured the coffee and handed it to the attractive young woman. "Here you go, Amber."

"Thank you."

The attractive, younger woman swiped her card and walked away. Tracy admired her as she walked, noticing her ample curves and her protruding backside. She thought to herself she would give anything to live her life for a bit, then went on helping the next customer in line.

Tracy's shift ended at noon and she sat in her car taking stock of her life before heading to Noah's house. She worked at a coffee shop at thirty-five, no children, no prospects for a husband, no family, and no friends, other than the few who hung around her to get high. She wondered why she ever let herself get hooked on the powder in the first place. She thought back to that day so long ago which started it all. Just out of high school, she and her long-time boyfriend wanted to experiment one night and try something new. She got hooked, he didn't. Shortly after, he broke it off with her and became a successful businessman who soon married and had a family. But not Tracy. She couldn't break her habit and soon everything she made went to support it. She aged and changed physically. No longer was she a plain yet pretty girl. The lines became clearer, the circles under her eyes darker, her breasts sagged, and her figure became boyish. She stayed with any man who'd have her just for shelter and structure in her life. Somehow, she was able to keep a job, although she'd been through five since she got hooked. Where was she headed? What would come of her once-promising life?

The new shipment was in and she wanted to grab a quarter G for the night. She texted Frankie before driving away: *I'm picking it up now, be over soon.*

Frankie responded: *Okay babe, see you soon. Let's snort and fuck.*

She read the last text in disgust. Frankie was a loser and she'd never have given him the time of day in her old life.

She pulled up to the huge stately colonial on the side of town she hardly ever visited, walked up to the door and knocked.

Noah, 12:15 pm...

The knock on the door came right on time at 12:15 pm. Noah came home for lunch just to make this transaction. He never dealt on weekends or nights, these times being when his family was around. His wife, Jamie, worked at the bank 9 am to 3 pm Tuesday through Thursday and his children were in school, so he fit all of his clients in during those times. He opened the door.

"Hello, Friday." He never used real names. He came up with Friday because she always wanted to get a fix for her weekend, so she came most Fridays.

"Hi, here's the forty," she said as she handed the handsome man an envelope.

"Thank you. Here's the quarter."

The girl took the fix and walked away without saying another word. Noah watched her go and felt a bit of sympathy. He closed the door and glanced at his watch. He had just enough time to grab lunch and make the scheduled tee-time of 1:30 pm. It was a bright warm day so he took the top down on his BMW four series convertible and headed to a local sports bar for a beer and some food. While eating, he took inventory of his life, which he did often. Assess, reassess, and adjust; that was the way to success in business and in life. He took out his phone and swiped through the pictures of his family: his beautiful wife, Alannah, and his two daughters, Emma and Abigail. They didn't know about his side project which supplemented his income enough to afford the stately house, the fancy cars, the trips, clothes, and private schooling for his daughters. His legitimate business of internet security was healthy and growing, however, not at the rate that would give he and his family what they wanted and needed. His illegitimate side project of selling cocaine covered the rest.

Noah finished his lunch and drove to his private golf course. He'd been a member for two years and he used the impressive clubhouse and well-kept course to close many of his past deals. Today was no different.

He met the Wilson brothers on the first tee and by the eighth tee, they were sold in purchasing his security for their new business website. After the glasses of expensive champagne, their handshakes and signatures were consummated.

Keith, 6:00 pm...

Keith and Carl signed the contract and drank their champagne before leaving the clubhouse. Keith felt Noah's security was just what his new business website needed. The business needed to grow exponentially, increasing every aspect as the sales increased. In the end, it was his decision. Apps-R-Us was his baby from the start and Carl had jumped aboard as an investor, a financial consultant, and shareholder. When you've created 25% of the newest apps on the internet, you need to protect them.

If only his home life were going as smoothly as his business. His twenty-one-year-old son, Joshua, had been in trouble his whole life. Joshua had been in and out of rehab, in and out of jail, with no job and no prospects. He knocked up a seventeen-year-old girl named Sadie who also was an addict without a steady job or a clue about life. Keith had never broken the law. However, this was his son's life at stake and the little bitch seemed unpersuadable; she was having Joshua's baby. She was four months pregnant and Keith knew she had no family and no connections. He, however, had someone who owed him a debt. Someone who knew the streets and how to get things done. He dialed his cell to take one more chance at solving the problem humanely.

"This is Johnny."

"Johnny, Keith. Have we made any progress with that thing?"

"Negative. She's not budging. I've threatened her with violence and with her life. This baby is her world. We need to move it along to plan two."

Keith closed his eyes. He hated what he was about to do but she left him no choice.

"Do it."

He disconnected the call before he had a chance to change his mind.

Johnny, 6:30 pm...

Johnny turned off his phone having received the green light to go ahead with plan two. He was glad, for plan two paid more money and he was far from caring about hurting people. He'd made a call to uncover some information on Sadie. She lived with two roommates, but he learned she'd be home alone this evening. It was amazing how fast you could discover any information you wanted to with money and the right connections.

Johnny drove by the site a few times before she arrived just to get the lay of the land. The sun had set beyond the horizon and darkness fell on the city. There was a lone car in the driveway. A few minutes later an attractive blonde woman walked out, jumped into the car, and drove off. Johnny smiled—it was time to earn his pay.

Sadie, 7:00 pm...

Sadie would babysit a couple of times a week to make some extra cash. She was trying to kick her drug addiction and save some money to prepare for her baby. The few clients she had knew nothing of her habit and she always did an exceptional job of caring for the little ones. She looked at it as practice for when her own baby came.

The mother and little boy had arrived right on time.

"Hi, Sadie, I'm sorry but I have to leave quickly. I have an appointment at seven pm."

"Well, you better go. It's already seven."

"He'll wait," the mom said with a wink. She then knelt to her child. "Be a good boy for Sadie, and remember I love you, Riley."

Riley, 7:15 pm...

The tragedy happened immediately after Amber drove away. A big, scary man kicked the door in and did something terrible to the nice girl who his mother left him with. He put a small gun to her head and pulled the trigger, sending half of her head across the room. Riley screamed. The man looked up, startled. Riley retracted away from the bad man, burying his face in the couch pillow. The man seemed to hesitate, seemingly deciding what the best course of action would be now. He bowed his head, gave the sign of the cross, and spoke softly to himself. "No loose ends." He aimed and pulled the trigger. Riley Williams was dead, four weeks shy of his fifth birthday.

THE END

AFTERWORD

Have you ever observed someone during the course of your typical day, maybe at the market, coffee shop, or just walking down the street and wondered *what's their story? Where are they going tonight? What secrets do they possess?* As a writer, my mind is full of curiosity and wonder and I sometimes create scenarios in my head about certain people I observe. This story is a result of that curious nature. We're all six degrees from our demise, so take every step cautiously; your life or the life of someone you love may depend on it.

KINDRED
SOULS

Norman Lewis was a simple man who enjoyed living his life with as few complications, connections, and relationships as possible. Men hated him, women hated him, children hated him, and even animals hated him. His beloved wife, Margaret, died over five years ago from a brain aneurysm. That was the day Norman cashed in his chips and gave up on life.

He lived alone in a small two-bedroom, one-bathroom house, the same house he and Margaret bought the year they were married. They lived there for fifty years before Margaret's sudden, somber passing. Before her death he was a happy, consistent man who loved his wife deeply. Margaret's inability to conceive children saddened her and made her feel like a failure in Norman's eyes, but Norman felt only love and admiration for her. Now, his blackened heart rotted in his chest and anyone or anything he could make enemies with, was a positive in his mind.

It was a bright, warm Sunday morning as Norman slowly sauntered down his walkway to the mailbox, hoping the delivery boy had gotten up early to deliver his Sunday paper. As he opened the empty mailbox he cursed the little shit. "Why you lazy, spoiled little brat. Would it kill you to get up before ten am?" As the words left his mouth, a rolled newspaper thumped him square in his forehead and fell to the concrete below. He heard a child's laughter ascending down the street as he looked up to catch the little bugger on his bike with his middle finger in the air, pointed at the old man.

"Damn parents let these little terrorists do whatever they wish," he mumbled as he picked up the paper and headed inside.

Jake sniffed around the empty garbage cans as his stomach ached from lack of food. The big truck had come this morning and emptied all of them. Foolishly, Jake missed the festivities because he'd fallen asleep on a bed of old newspapers in his favorite alley downtown. He decided he'd try a few more cans before heading to the park to beg for scraps as the friendly families ate their lunches. Jake had been homeless and living on the street for over a year. He missed Tommy, the little boy who claimed him at the pound. Jake had screwed up as usual and peed one too many times in the house. Tommy's dad had enough and drove him to the other side of town and let him go. Jake thought about Tommy all the time. He was his best friend.

Jake was a mutt, a mix of too many breeds to tell what he actually was. He was a plain brown color with plain brown eyes. He wasn't a good watch dog, he wasn't attractive, and he sure as heck wasn't overly intelligent. He was just a small dog who wanted to find a family to call his own. As he trotted down the street, cars honked at him as people yelled for him to get out of the way, so he cantered onto the sidewalk, safe from the angry automobiles. Jake spent another full day without food and his ribs started to show. He wondered why Tommy let his father do this to him.

Norman exercised his usual weekend ritual of sitting at his kitchen table nursing his black morning coffee while reading the paper until the Red Sox game aired at 1:00 pm. The days seemed to blend together, without any divergent to break up the monotony of his life. This is what he'd become, and he was fine with it. Someday soon he'd pass. They'd stumble on his cold body, still sitting in his recliner in front of his television set. Norman Lewis had accepted his fate and his slow decline into nothingness.

Norman was reading a political article on the editorial page. It seemed the writer supported gay marriage, raising the minimum wage, and expressed his concern over the rights of the transgender.

"What the...?"

What happened to the simplicity of life? When men married women and they had children. When people made money directly related to their merit. When you didn't need to run an algorithm to figure out which restroom someone should use. I just don't understand this world anymore...

A loud crash came from the front of the house, pulling him out of his intellectual thought. He dropped the paper and walked to the living room. There, sitting in the middle of the floor, was a rock. It had violated his home through the front window, which was now shattered into a thousand pieces of glass. He walked to the opening that forty seconds ago contained his window and peered out. He saw two youngsters just as they were entering the woods across the street, obviously running from the scene of their crime.

Why? Why are people so mean? Why are they so mean to me?

The park was crawling with people and more were on their way. The sun shone brilliantly and what remained of the sparse morning clouds evaporated, leaving a bright blue hue to the sky. Jake sauntered around hoping to find some scraps on the ground or a nice family to feed him. He trotted by a well-manicured poodle on a leash with her loving family close by. She glanced at him and quickly turned her nose up and looked away. Strays had no respect in the canine hierarchy. If you were of any value or class, you were owned by a human. Jake found a wrapper with some cheese around the edges on the ground and he quickly licked up the golden goodness. He continued on, passing a chatty Chihuahua wearing a gem studded collar. Her owner was an attractive, well-dressed female who gave her a piece of meat that a male human had cooked on a grill. They offered none to Jake, so he went on his way. It was then a park employee noticed Jake and started toward him with a long stick with a loop at the end. Jake had seen these contraptions many times and knew the imminent danger they represented. Jake broke into a full gallop and headed for a small thicket of trees that bordered a small wooded area. He continued through the grove to the other side, turning back to make sure he lost the bad man. He came upon a little boy who was enjoying a hotdog as his family played frisbee close by. He looked at Jake and held out his hand. Jake licked his fingers and the boy pet him on top of his head. The positive physical contact felt invigorating and Jake sat back and looked the boy in the eyes. The boy held out what was left of his hotdog and Jake gently took it from his hand, being sure not to clip a finger with his teeth.

The boy's mother yelled as she hurried over, "Cage! Get the hell away from that stray! Who knows where he's been or what kind of disease he's carrying!" When she got to them, she snipped, "Get away, you dirty mutt!" as she smacked Jake on top of the head with her frisbee, which sent Jake scurrying away. From a safe distance, he stopped and glanced back at the boy who waved goodbye to him. Jake dropped his head, turned away, and continued his lonely trek.

Norman cooked himself grilled cheese for Sunday dinner, just the way Margaret used to make it. When full, he poured himself an iced tea, lit up his pipe, and sat out on the back deck to watch the sun go down and the moon rise. He glanced around the backyard and took inventory of what needed to be done. The grass needed another cut soon, the shrubs needed trimming, and the flower beds needed to be weeded. Norman really didn't care much for flowers, but Margaret loved them and always had a beautiful garden of Perennials. Norman continued the tradition after she passed. He needed to keep as much of her alive as possible. He found comfort in the little reminders he stumbled upon every day.

Norman crawled into bed at his usual time of 9:00 pm and started reading a new book. He soon grew weary and turned off the night-light, placed the book on the night-stand, and waited for sleep to come. His mind wandered as he tossed and turned. He glanced at Margaret's pillow on the right side of the bed and the empty space that his wife's body had occupied. A tear fell as he was overtaken with grief, still, five years later. He was lonely and sad, but that's the way he wanted it as every attempt form anyone to enter his life was rejected and pushed away. The stoic, masculine man of seventy-five years who was a soldier for over ten of them, cried himself to sleep once again.

Jake scavenged enough food throughout the day to calm his hunger and now was searching for a safe, quiet place to rest for the evening. His alleyway was on the other side of town and he was exhausted, so he stayed in the park and found a thicket of shrubs with a canopy that would shelter him from the rain and also camouflage him from any imminent danger. He curled up on a warm patch of weeds and lay his head on his front paws. He was instantly asleep as the long day had taken its toll on his little body. Dreams of food, Tommy, and sleeping in a warm bed came quickly.

Norman arose early on Monday morning. It was a bright, sunny start to the day, so Norman planned to attack the backyard chores that were in desperate need of attention. After brewing a pot of freshly ground coffee—another one of Margaret's favorite small indulgences—he headed into the backyard where he spent the next three hours catching up on his landscaping.

At noon, he decided to head into town and grab lunch a few miles down the main road at the local dinner which he frequented two or three times a week. He pulled up to a stop light and waited for the illusive green light to show its face. He glanced to the sidewalk and noticed a mangy, stray with its tongue hanging out, seemingly searching for something, probably food. He made a mental note to call the dog officer to have the dirty mutt taken away. The light finally turned and he went on his way.

He pulled his white Impala into the diner parking lot, grabbed a science magazine off the passenger seat and took his usual seat in the corner by the window. Ten minutes later, the waitress sauntered over.

"What'll it be today, old-timer? The usual, meatloaf?"

"Yes, please. With milk."

The middle-aged woman rolled her eyes before turning to place his order. Norman didn't know why she hated him. Norman didn't understand much about society these days. It was a fast-growing world, moving in many new, extravagant directions, and he couldn't keep up or understand it all. He felt alone and left out, like he was still living the world of three decades ago.

While waiting for his food, he opened the magazine to an article on assisted dying in the Netherlands. Seems the Dutch government intended to draft a law legalizing assisted suicide for people who feel they've "completed life." The article gave a web address and a phone number which Norman quickly jotted down.

"Here you go. Anything else?' the waitress asked as she placed his plate in front of him.

"No, that'll be it, thank you."

She just walked away. No *you're welcome* or *have a good day.* He glanced up and saw her behind the counter on her phone as another customer struggled to get her attention. When had society become so rude?

Norman ate his lunch and headed home for his afternoon nap.

Jake continued his journey down the busy main street headed away from the park without any real destination. He was doing what all canines do; follow their nose. He paused to sniff around a small wooden area when a white car pulled into the driveway across the street. Jake sat still as an older man exited the vehicle and looked in his direction. Something in the man's eyes, a flash or a gleam, caught Jake's attention and he kept watching as the man stepped inside his house. Some instinct inside his canine brain told him to stay here for the rest of the day as he found a cool patch of green grass to lay in.

Norman watched the stray mutt across the street. He seemed to be hanging around for some reason and Norman picked up the phone to call the pound. He dialed and waited for an answer.

"Hello, west-side dog pound."

"Hel—."

Before he continued speaking something caught his attention. A look in the dog's eyes, maybe, or just a feeling of human decency. He hung the phone up before reporting the culprit. All day long Norman kept his eye on the ugly stray and all day long the mutt stayed in the wooded lot. Norman called the assisted suicide hot-line and the receptionist said she would email him an application. They went over the particulars: the cost, which was of no concern to Norman, the location, and how they actually went about the process. It seems you stayed at this beautiful resort on a beach for a week. On the final day, they administer euthanasia medication and you fade away with the pleasant memories of that week in the foremost of your brain. It all sounded fabulous to Norman. He planned to fill out the application and be off this earth within a month's time.

Jake camped out in the wooded lot for the night and arose with the sun the following morning. He noticed the man's house was still quiet without any movement, so he ventured across the street onto the front walk. He sat there looking at the front door until he tired and stretched his body out on the warm cement.

An hour later the door opened and the old man walked onto his front steps, keeping his eyes on Jake the whole time.

"What do you want? Scram, you filthy beast." Jake just looked at him. "Go on, get away. Find another place to hang out."

For some reason, Jake ignored the man's malevolence and remained. He saw past the open display of contempt and noticed a kindness and a warmth hiding beneath the surface. It was a sense only a canine's instincts could hone in on. Throughout the day, the man would check on him, shooing him away every time. However, Jake was stubborn and stayed. By nighttime, Jake's hunger kicked in and he became weak. The door flew open suddenly and the man walked out down the steps and stopped just short of Jake.

"Here. I'm only doing this once, so after you're finished, please be on your way." The man tossed some leftover steak in Jake's general direction. It was the most delicious meal Jake had ever tasted. When finished, he sat up with his tongue hanging out and his tail wagging.

"That's all I have, now be gone," the man said as he retreated up the steps. As he opened the door to enter, Jake saw something that he would dream about throughout the night. The man smiled. It was just a quick, slight smile, but it was there.

Norman woke up to the sun's bright rays coming through his bedroom window. He rose, threw on his robe, and headed for the kitchen to brew a pot of coffee. As he passed the front window, he remembered the stray dog from the previous evening. He glanced out and noticed the mutt was still there, curled up on the soft grass just off the walkway. Though Norman prided himself on being a tough, unfeeling individual, feelings of sympathy and guilt passed through him as he made his way to the kitchen.

After pouring a mug of coffee and placing his scrambled eggs and toast on a plate, he sat at the dining room table to enjoy his breakfast. The fluffy, sweet eggs hit the spot and the smooth, nutty taste of the coffee reminded him that there were still experiences to remain alive for and enjoy. The pleasant moment quickly passed though, and he was slipping back into his depressed, lonely state of mind within minutes. A few mouthfuls of eggs remained but before shoveling the rest into his mouth, his thoughts returned to the living, breathing animal in his front yard. He picked up the plate and walked out the front door. The canine looked up at the commotion. Norman reached down and left the plate at the end of the walk, just off the front stoop. He turned and headed back inside to fire up his computer.

He read the application and electronically signed and dated it. He paused for just a moment before hitting send. The application was on its way and Norman had taken another step toward ending his morbid life.

Norman had fallen asleep in front of the television. Glancing at the clock and noticing it was mid-afternoon, he rushed to his computer to see if he'd received a response from the assisted suicide people.

Dear Mr. Norman Lewis,

We've reviewed your application and have determined you're a suitable client for our program. As a matter of fact, you're exactly the type of client we have based our enterprise on. We have set up a suite for you on the date of August 2nd, where you'll spend a week relaxing and enjoying your last days until the culmination of your life on August 9th. Please fill out the attached questionnaire and we'll make all the arrangements for your funeral and burial wishes. Once we've received the funds discussed in the application, the process is complete, and your suite and salvation day will be booked.

Best wishes,

Paradise awaits

Norman re-read the email and sat back to brood over his decision. Much of his estate would go into this endeavor, so he wanted to make sure it was what he wanted before wiring the money. Without warning, a thought of the dog came into his mind. He walked to the front window and looked out. The mutt was sitting on the walk just staring at the front door. The plate had been licked clean. Norman opened the door, stepped out, and reached down to pick it up. Before turning to go back in, he crouched down and made a clicking noise toward the dog. The mutt inched towards him with his ears back and a small wag of his tail. Norman held out his hand and the dog sniffed and looked up into his eyes before giving his hand a warm, wet lick. He noticed an old, worn collar with a metal tag. He reached down and turned the tag over in his hand. "Jake," he said as he read the engraved tag. Norman pet him once on the top of his head before returning inside to wire the money.

Jake licked his lips, savoring the delicious taste of the food the kind human had shared with him. The man's scent reminded him of Tommy's; it was the scent of home, calming and pure. Jake knew now more than ever this was his last stand. He'd live or die with the kind man with the soothing scent.

Norman couldn't hit the send button. He sat in front of his computer, his finger hovering over the enter button. His mind remained on the new friend he'd made on his front walk. He took his hand away, pushed the chair back, and stood.

The dog was still there, his eyes fixed on the front door. Out on the street, a dog catcher who'd been routinely cruising the neighborhood pulled up and exited his vehicle, starting toward Jake. Norman sighed and opened the door. He called out, "Here Jake, here, boy!" Jake wagged his tail with his soft eyes on Norman as the officer approached the scene.

"Sir, is this your dog?"

"Yes, I'm sorry officer, he got out accidentally."

"Okay, please take better care of keeping him leashed, we had two calls on him today. Next time I'll have to write out a citation."

"I understand. Have a great day, officer." Norman reached down and pet Jake. As the man drove away, Norman called, "Here boy, come." Jake hesitated momentarily before following him inside. Jake heard the door click shut behind him and he took in what he hoped would become his new home.

That evening, Norman made a trip to the pet store. He purchased pet shampoo, a flea collar, a leash, and a week's supply of dog food. Jake rode shotgun with his nose pointed out the open window, the clean, crisp air blowing through his sinuses and his tail wagging in complete bliss. Jake had experienced a few rides in the past when Tommy's mother had allowed him to join the family, but mostly remained home because Tommy's father didn't want the dog ruining the interior of his vehicles. It was everything he remembered and more. Every so often he would turn to Norman with his tongue hanging out in a gesture of thanks for including him in the festivities. Norman would always respond with a quick pat on his back.

When they returned home, Norman led Jake into the bathroom to prepare for a bath. Jake stood in the tub as the warm, soapy water soothed him and felt glorious on his dirty, matted fur. He'd been programmed to hate the water as the rains he endured as a stray were cold and made it impossible to find a comfortable place to lay, but this experience was the total opposite. When done, Norman towel dried him, placed his new collar around his neck, and fed him some of the food. Jake swallowed in gulps as his stomach yearned to be full for the first time in many days. When he was done eating, the pair sat out on the back deck and admired the fenced-in yard and the warm, beautiful summer night with its bright stars shining through an ebony sky. Norman noticed how much better Jake looked with some food in his stomach and his freshly washed coat. He lit a pipe and Jake lay beside him, his world on this day having turned out perfect.

Jake had slept beside Norman's bed and the pair were up early together. Norman made coffee and breakfast and fed Jake some dog food. He then hooked Jake's new leash onto his collar and headed for the front door.

"Jake, want to go for a walk?"

Jake remembered the word from the few times Tommy had said it and knew it meant going outside. He panted and wagged his tail faster as they stepped outside into a beautiful, bright morning. The rising sun had just broken the horizon and an orange glow filled the eastern portion of the sky. The pair stooped to admire it momentarily before going on their way.

A few streets south they approached the paperboy on his bike. The boy stopped and dropped his papers as he hopped off his bike.

"Hi, mister! Can I pet him?"

David Boiani

"Sure, Jake is very friendly."

Jake licked the boy's hand which brought a giggle from the youngster. "He's a cool dog, do you walk him every morning?"

"I will be from now on."

"Cool, I'm on this route every day, I'll see you guys tomorrow."

The boy picked his bag up, jumped back on his bike and was gone.

When they returned from the walk, Norman checked his computer and noticed one new email.

Hi, Norman Lewis,

We haven't received your payment for your reserved week and consequent procedure. We must receive the funds within seven days of your acceptance or you will lose your reservation.

Hope to hear from you soon,

Director Martin Lawrence

Norman re-read the email and contemplated his next action. He leaned forward and hit delete then turned the computer off. Norman Lewis wasn't ready to die yet. Jake needed him, and suddenly he had a purpose in life.

Days passed and Jake and Norman became family. Norman installed a pet door leading to the backyard for Jake to use whenever he needed to empty his bladder or bowels. They continued their daily rituals of morning walks, hanging out in the backyard at sunset, and sleeping together. Norman had finally allowed Jake in the bed with him after he solved his flea problem. Jake had recovered from lack of nourishment to become an attractive, healthy dog. The paper boy had frequently started coming by with his friends to visit Jake and Norman. Norman had learned his name, Brain Peterson. Brain was over early one evening and the three friends sat on the back deck, sipping lemonade.

"Norman, I think it's so cool that you saved Jake's life. He'd probably be dead or in the pound right now if you didn't take him in," Brian said.

"Son, it may look like I saved this dog, but believe me, he saved me."

"How?"

"Let's just say we are kindred spirits."

"What does kindred mean?"

"Related, connected, meant to be together."

"Hmmm, I see. Norman, there's something I need to tell you that I feel pretty bad about."

"It was you and your friends who threw the rock through my window, right?"

"But...how did you know?"

"I've always known, son. Old doesn't mean stupid."

"I'm sorry."

"Apology accepted. That was a lifetime ago. Many things have changed since then."

"Thanks. You really are a cool dude for an old guy." Brian stood up. "I have to get going. Mom wants me home as soon as the street lights come on."

"Wow, parents still use that one, huh? That goes back to my childhood."

"They had streetlights back then?"

"Watch it, kid, or you won't be seeing my generous tips in your envelope on Sunday morning."

Brian laughed, petted Jake one last time and walked out as he said, "See you guys tomorrow."

"Have a good night."

Soon after, Norman and Jake went inside and headed upstairs to bed.

Weeks passed, the early autumn weather rolled in and Norman was enjoying his pipe on the sofa after a long walk with Jake. Jake had been sleeping at his friend's feet when he was woken by a strange smell and smoke billowing through the air. He lifted his head to see Norman asleep and his pipe spilled onto the floor on the other side of the couch. The carpet had caught ablaze and the modest, adolescent flames were growing quickly and spreading across the floor. Jake immediately jumped up and barked at the old man, attempting to wake him, but he remained deep asleep as the smoke moved in around them both. Jake grabbed Norman's pant leg in his mouth and pulled with all the strength he had. As Norman tumbled over and off the couch his eyes flew open and his face showed shock in what was happening around him. Norman jumped up and followed Jake, who was waiting for him at the front door. The room was filled with smoke and the old man struggled to get the door opened as both he and Jake inhaled the dark, thick smoke. Finally, the door pulled open and they escaped as the flames chased them down. Sirens wailed as firetrucks and ambulances pulled up in front of the house. Because of the smoke they had inhaled, both man and canine collapsed on the front lawn, lying motionless.

Norman and Brian bowed their heads in somber memory of Jake before Brian began shoveling dirt into the grave in Norman's backyard. The boy's tears fell freely as his view of the wooden coffin slowly became smaller with each shovelful. When the hole was completely filled in, the boy hugged Norman and cried into his shirt.

"Why did it have to happen to Jake! Why?"

"It's the way the world works, Brian. There are many evil things that happen we simply cannot control."

"But why would God let it happen?"

Norman just held the boy to him. He didn't have the heart to say, "Because there is no God, son..."

There is no God. No God...no God...

Norman shot up, sweat pouring off his chin. "What? Where?"

"Well, look who decided to join us," a pretty nurse said from the corner of the hospital room.

"What happened? Where am I?"

"You're in Harmony General Hospital. You're lucky to be alive. You inhaled some smoke and have a few first degree burns, but other than that, you'll be fine. How does your throat feel?"

Norman swallowed. "Fine."

"That's great news. You don't have any symptoms or show any signs of serious injury to your throat or lungs. You're very lucky, Mr. Lewis."

"Jake? Where's my dog?"

"He was taken to the veterinarian. He's fine. A Brian Pederson waited for the results at the clinic when he was brought in unconscious, just like yourself. He wanted to take him home and care for him, but he needed veterinarian care and he would need a waiver from you for them to release him."

"Where's Jake now?"

"Still at the clinic."

"Get me the waiver. I want him to go home with Brian."

"Sure, I believe I have it in your personal effects. Let me check. I'll be right back."

The nurse returned with the paperwork and Norman signed the release before drifting off to sleep. Only pleasant dreams came.

In the following days Norman thought about life and if the relationships we make happen because of destiny or just plain luck. Was Jake inserted into his life by some type of divine intervention or was it just happenstance? Right place... Right time. Was there a predetermined path each of us take or do we all just float around as victims of chaos theory, our paths constantly changing depending on our decisions, which way the wind blows, or the flap of a butterflies' wings on the other side of the planet? Maybe *not* understanding is how it should be. Maybe, if we knew all the answers, we'd walk around miserable, having nothing more to learn or explore.

Whether nature or higher power, the design and application seem to work. People needed mysteries. All Norman really knew was Jake had become an integral part of his life and however that came to be, he was happy it happened. He fell asleep that night staring at the moon through his hospital room window, pondering life's unknowns.

Norman was released a few days later. As the cab pulled up to the front of his house, he saw Brain and his friends waiting for him. In the middle of the group of boys sat an impatient brown dog, his tongue out and his tailing pounding a hole in the ground. When he saw Norman, he ran full speed toward his master and friend jumping into the man's arms. As the canine licked his face, Norman kissed the top of Jake's head and said, "I love you, boy, and I promise, no more pipes." Jake let out a small bark, showing the man he understood, and the kindred souls headed up the walkway to the waiting boys.

The End

AFTERWORD

I believe some events happen at just the right moment between just the right parties which changes the course of their lives forever. I don't believe things happen for a "reason," or predetermined destinies, as there are far too many variables involved to accept one explanation for where our lives end up. However, sometimes the odds are beaten and something magical happens. Two people fall in a love which lasts forever. Two people meet and create a true friendship which survives the test of time. This story was written to display the magic that's alive in this world, and sometimes, we get just what we need at just the right time.

UNIT 913

Louisiana, spring, 2015

The cell bars slammed shut as three guards lead John Bard to the interrogation room. He felt the eyes of his brethren on him as he passed each cell. John kept his eyes down. As a dead man walking for the crimes he committed, he found it hard to look other inmates in the eyes. It was almost as if he'd accepted defeat to the system. Guards were a different story—he could stare them down all day.

They entered the room and the guards shackled him to the chair by the far end of the table. When he was secured, his lawyer Tom Lepinstein walked in followed by a couple of serious looking men in black suits. When they were all seated, one of the two agents spoke.

"John, this is my partner, James Herron and I'm William Harris. We're agents of the C.I.A."

"Sure, so what the fuck do you want?" John said as he glanced at Lepinstein who kept a stern, blank look on his face.

"You're scheduled to be executed in October," Harris said as he shuffled through his notes more for show than anything. "We're here to offer you an alternative."

"Alternative? Go on..."

"How would you like not just a stay of execution, but to be a free man?"

Bard looked from one to the other and back again before raising his eyebrows. He turned to his lawyer.

"John, these men want to offer you a deal for your life. Listen to the offer and we can discuss it after."

Bard nodded and waved his hand for the men in black to continue.

"We want you to be part of an experiment. An experiment which may serve the safety and defense of this country, forever." Harris glanced at Herron with a smirk on his face. "Imagine that, you can go from a hated public enemy to a patriot with one signature."

"Fuck you, I ain't some guinea pig."

"I'll be honest, Bard, it repulses me to sit here and talk to you like you're a decent human being. You've raped and murdered over ten women. You disgust me, but I'm here for the well-being of this country, the country I love. I'm offering you a second chance at life. Sign the document, join in the experiment, go free. But there's one catch. You must leave the country when it's over, no exceptions. We'll hunt you down if you stay."

"Join the experiment? Does that mean I won't be alone?"

Harris glanced at Herron who gave a slight nod.

"You'll be joining two others who've already accepted."

"Who are they?"

"Voss Hallwell and Nasir Shekau. We'll be testing a new drug for use on our future soldiers. It creates immense strength, infinite endurance, and extinguishes all fear."

"Hallwell is that pedophile, correct?"

"Yes."

"Who's the other?"

The agents glanced at each other, Herron gave Harris a slight nod.

"He was arrested on allegations of having ties to a terrorist organization on American soil."

"Any proof?"

"We cannot discuss his case with you."

Bard gave Harris a wry smile. "So, how do I know you won't just kill me after?"

"We all sign a government document binding us to the agreement. Obama signs it himself, although I'm sure he won't be thrilled about his signature sharing the page with yours."

Bard looked at Harris and grinned.

"So, what's the experiment?"

"A new drug our scientists have invented. It's a hallucinogen. It creates immense strength, infinite endurance, and extinguishes all fear. Once you're finished with your thirty days on the drug, you're free to go."

"What's the drug for?"

Harris smiled and looked around the cold, grey room.

"Isn't it obvious? Soldiers who are overflowing with energy that don't require sleep. Workers building our planes, tanks, ships, and submarines who'll be inviolable, creating super-efficient warriors who'll build the countries' defensive machinery, materials, and weaponry at a rate far greater than they are currently. The possibilities are endless. We've tested the drug on animals and now it's time to push through to the next step."

"What if it has no effect on me? What if it fails? Would that void the contract?"

"It won't."

Bard once again searched the faces of the two men before replying, "Give me a few to talk it over with my legal counsel."

"Of course, take as long as you'd like."

Minutes later the contract was signed. John Bard was led out of the room and back to his cell with thoughts of freedom dancing in his head.

Harris turned to Herron with a concerned look on his face but before he could utter a word Herron put his hand up and said, "Bill, there is no way this government will let any of them walk. It'll be taken care of."

Harris nodded, smiled and the two men shook hands and left the prison.

Parts unknown, autumn, 2015

The three test subjects were transported in a military bus to the experiment facility, otherwise known as unit 913. Military soldiers escorted the trio into a 25' by 25' chamber with hoods over their heads. John Bard was led to a couch. He took a seat as the soldiers removed his hood. Soon after the other two test subjects joined him. Doctor Reinheart was escorted into the chamber.

"Hello, gentlemen, welcome to unit 913. This will be your home for the next month, and if you successfully complete the experiment, you will be set free. Now on to the procedure. This chamber will be sealed from the outside world. No way in, no way out. The entry door will remain locked at all times. We'll survey you from behind the four portholes on the far wall."

John Bard looked around the room he'd be living in for the next thirty days. There were three cots with no bedding, just a place to lay, but not to sleep. There was one bathroom with a toilet and shower stall which they'd obviously share. A couple of couches, chairs, bookcase filled with books and board games, and a dining table and chairs filled out the chamber. That's all the room contained.

"We'll serve you three meals a day through the middle port hole which can be opened from the outside to pass articles through. That's the only contact you'll have with us. The drug will be chemically added to your food and water. It has no flavor or color. This drug, called hallucinogen #13, will change the way you think, feel and live throughout your stay here. You will not feel pain, you'll have unlimited energy, and you won't require much sleep. I hope this experiment finds you well and we all can benefit from it. Now, any questions?"

John looked at his two roommates. Hallwell was a wiry older man who looked the part of a pedophile. His beady eyes looked through you instead of at you. He was thin, maybe 150 pounds, and stood nearly six feet. He had thinning grey hair that needed a wash and his movements were fidgety and jumpy, as if he were always trying to get away with something evil. Nasir Shekau was large for a Muslim, standing over six feet. However, unlike Hallwell, he was thick and muscular, as if he had spent the last four years in captivity pumping iron.

"I have a question," Bard asked.

Reinheart nodded in his direction to proceed.

"What if these two ass-wipes get on my nerves?"

"Please, try to get along with each other. It'll make your stay so much more bearable. Anything else?"

The trio remained quiet, so Reinheart left the chamber followed by his posse of soldiers.

Bard looked at his two partners, shrugged his shoulders and spread out on the couch. Suddenly they heard noise coming from the far wall. It was first meal being presented through the portholes and Bard let out a chuckle and placed his hands behind his head.

Day one

Test subject one: Bard
Bard seems to be the leader of the group. He's the most outgoing and aggressive.

Test subject two: Hallwell
Quiet and definitely a follower. He has a creepy way about him that Bard has definitely picked up on.

Test subject three: Shekau
An introvert with hidden inner strength. He seems less likely to follow Bard's lead.

Conclusion:
It'll be interesting to see how the hierarchy is affected as periods of time elapse.

The first few days the subjects live amongst themselves without issue. They eat, drink, read without uttering a word to each other. They show no ill effects of sleep deprivation. On the third day, the subjects converse about their prior lives. Bard pulls the chessboard down from the bookcase, sets up a game and speaks: "Okay, which of you two creeps is going to lose to me in chess?"

Hallwell is silent. Shekau, however, steps forward. "I know of this game. I have played many times."

"Well, sit your Muslim ass down and dig in, my friend. If we have to be here, we may as well do our best to enjoy the stay."

As the third day passed, Hallwell starts to become jumpy. He can't sit still and walks around the other two while they play on. Finally, he sits in the corner of the room by himself and pulls his pants down to masturbate. Bard losses it.

"What the fuck!" He jumps up and approaches one of the ports. "Get this sick fuck out of here. I won't watch him pull on his dick!"

Nasir Shekau remains calm. "Bard, sit and play. Let him be by himself."

Day three ended with Hallwell having a silent orgasm while the other two move their chess pieces across the board as they continue their play.

On day four, Nasir Shekau uses a chess piece to carve four gashes in the wall. He seems to be keeping pace of time by the rhythm of the meals being served to them.

Day five

Test subject one: Bard

Bard lost the chess game to Shekau. Then lost the rematch. As the third game took form, Bard realized he was rapidly losing again and threw the board against the wall. I feel this was a combination of the drug and his uncontrollable temper, which arises when he doesn't get what he wants.

Test subject two: Hallwell

Hallwell is by far the weakest of the group and I expect him to crack fairly early in the process. We'll need to decipher our soldiers and understand which will be able to endure the effects of the drugs.

Test subject three: Shekau

Shekau is by far the most interesting of the group. He's quiet, like Hallwell, but far more controlled. He doesn't seem to possess the outward angst and aggression that Bard displays. However, he seems to thrive on psychological torture as stated in his file. He had survived many years of torture from the U.S. Government, not just physical, but mental. They'd tell him his parents had died, that his wife moved on and became pregnant by another man, (which happened to be true) and/or go as far as telling him his baby that he had never met died in an accident. I noticed that when Bard lost it and threw the game board across the room, Shekau smiled and watched in pleasure.

Conclusion:

The drug's effects have definitely begun to affect Bard and Hallwell, but Shekau stills shows no effects. He's the type of man this program was created for.

At five days the two subjects, Bard and Hallwell, start to demonstrate paranoia. They stop talking and pace the room like caged animals mumbling to themselves. Hallwell sneaks up to the mirrored port-holes and pleads with whoever is behind the glass to, "Please, let me out. These two are planning an escape. Let me out and I'll tell you how."

On the seventh day, Hallwell starts screaming and runs back and forth from wall to wall. Bard whispers into the microphones. The scientists cannot make out what he says.

On the eight day, Hallwell rips out his own vocal chords. The other two just watch him as if they were enjoying a pleasant day at the park. Blood pours from his throat and the doctor has to decide whether to intervene and give him medical attention but, in the end, they stick to the plan of not intervening in the experiment. This would be the final decision going forward. Let things play out naturally. It was the only way to determine whether the gas would prove effective and what adjustments would have to be made in the drug itself and its dosages. Hallwell would never speak again, even if he survived and was granted his freedom. Shekau keeps up his habit of keeping count of the days on the wall. He's carved eight gashes with a chess piece.

On the ninth day, there was silence from the chamber. Bard quietly smears his own feces on the wall. Hallwell watches and mimics laughter without actually making a sound, and Shekau just sits and watches as if he was at a midnight showing of the movie of the week.

All of them seem to be filled with an intensity and strength, with Shekau the least affected at this point.

On the tenth day, Bard urinates on Hallwell who gets down on the floor and opens his mouth to drink it. Bard screeches a high-pitched laughter, almost as if from a man who has lost his mind entirely. Still, Shekau watches in silence. At this point, all three subjects have ceased sleeping.

Day ten

Test subject one: Bard
Bard's eating has slowed and has ceased any communication with his chamber-mates. Only a third of the way through the experiment, I don't see him having the resolve to make it to the end with his mind intact. He's displayed inhuman strength, once picking up the couch by himself and heaving it at the locked door.

Test subject two: Hallwell
Hallwell is by far in the worst shape of the three. Whether the smaller body structure has something to do with it, I do not know. It's more likely he just isn't as mentally strong as the other two.

Test subject three: Shekau
Shekau has been the least affected by the drug. He's also slept the least of the group, probably a result of his superior physical conditioning. He mostly just sits and observes but shows no sign of losing his mind like Hallwell and to a lesser extent, Bard.

Conclusion:
I'm disappointed how quickly Hallwell has lost touch with reality. Bard seems to have started that same slide, but I'm impressed with the continued resolve of Shekau. If we can find a way to perfect the gas and the dosage to give our soldiers, it could change war as we know it.

On day twelve, Hallwell licks off Bard's decaying feces from the walls. Bard sits in the corner and rocks back and forth like an autistic toddler. Shekau has started smiling. Just a calm, innocent smile as he continues to observe his fellow test subjects. They continue to receive food and drink through the port-holes.

Day thirteen. Shekau rises, walks over to the portholes, looks directly into them and smiles. His smile starts to take a sinister look, however, as if he's started his downward spiral into hallucinogenic insanity.

Day fourteen. Hallwell starts ripping chunks of flesh off his body and shoving them into his mouth. He has begun eating himself alive.

On day fifteen, Bard joins in and begins pulling loose flesh off Hallwell and eating it. Hallwell's thighs are all but gone and the pair starts ripping into his torso. Shekau picks up the chess pieces one by one and spends hours examining each of them.

Day fifteen

Test subjects one and two: Bard and Hallwell
Exactly halfway through, it's evident that both Hallwell and Bard have lost their minds. I'll no longer continue to monitor and log a file on these two.

Test subject three: Shekau
I'm very intrigued by Shekau's toughness, resolve, and resistance to the drug's effects. My question now is, what makes him different?

Conclusion:
I'll continue to monitor Shekau and try to define the differences in the test subjects. If I can bottle that, I can change the world.

Day sixteen and Hallwell is almost dead. He's prone on his back on the floor. Blood has pooled and dried underneath him, and every now and then he lets out a morbid groan. He and Bard have picked his flesh to the bone on his legs and they've dug holes into his chest and abdomen.

Day Seventeen. Hallwell is gone. Bard is having a feast on his body. He continues to rip out flesh from Hallwell's torso. His ribcage is now fully exposed.

Day eighteen. Shekau walks over to the portholes and shows a chess piece to the mirrored glass. He then points to the piece and at his chest. It's the King piece. He smiles and throws it at the glass and walks away, back to his corner.

On day nineteen, Bard rips out Hallwell's eyes and eats them like gumdrops. He exists in his own world now. He seldom even notices Shekau is in the chamber with him. Every now and then, he glances at him with a hollow look in his eyes.

Day twenty. Bard has started ripping his own flesh from his body, starting at the thighs, just like Hallwell.

Day twenty

I'm sickened by what has gone on in the chamber. Two of my men have vomited while monitoring when I was away from the portholes. It's stuff from a nightmare. I'm considering ending the experiment early. However, I'm still intrigued by just how long Shekau can remain sane. He continues to eat the food hungrily, which is remarkable considering how he's kept his composure even with the immense intake of the drug. I can only imagine the smell in that room. I've recorded the results up to this point and have learned from them. Adjustments will be made prior to the next experiment. I'll need to isolate the positive effects while deleting the negative ones for the drug to achieve its intended results.

Day twenty-one. Since Bard has started eating himself. It won't be long before he has passed, just like Hallwell. Shekau watches him with interest and continues to nourish his body with the food and water provided.

On day twenty-two, Bard rips his own eyes from their sockets and greedily swallows them down. Shekau observes this spectacle without any response at all, as if this were an everyday occurrence.

Day twenty-three. Bard has been reduced to a pile of flesh which lays on the floor barely still alive. He's ripped open his torso, just as Hallwell did. His eye sockets are a crimson mix of flesh and blood, seeping down his cheeks. He cannot get up as his leg muscles are gone, as he's torn them away and eaten them. Shekau keeps his day count on the wall with twenty-three gashes.

Day twenty-four. Bard is dead. Shekau seems happier now that he's alone. He smiles and stares at the wall. He uses the toilet to release a bowel movement and wipes himself with toilet paper, as if personal hygiene still matters in the horrific, bloody, stinking abyss he's living in.

On day twenty-five Shekau showers. He looks half-dead, his eyes are bright red and bloodshot, he's lost significant weight in muscle tone, but his mind still seems to be strong and free. He steps out of the shower, brushes his hair then blows a kiss towards the port-holes.

Day twenty-five

I have no explanation as to how our final test subject can remain so sane in comparison to the other two. The two guards stationed with me here have actually begun rooting for him, this Muslim captive accused of terrorist connections and schemes. His strength and perseverance have inspired these men, as he is now viewed as an underdog overcoming substantial odds.

Day twenty-six. For the first time, Shekau has paid some attention to the two mutilated corpses he shares his chamber with. He kneels down beside Hallwell and runs his hands over his torso with his back to the port-holes.

David Boiani

Day twenty-seven. Shekau sits facing a corner of the chamber with something in his hands, not visible to the observers.

Day twenty-eight. Shekau takes a break from sitting in the corner with his back to the port-holes to carve his twenty-eight gash in the wall.

Day twenty-nine. Shekau stands in front of the port-holes all day with a broad smile on his face which says: "I have won."

Day thirty. Shekau sits in the middle of the room with his hands parted and raised to the sky, his head thrown back and his eyes closed, as if he is in a deep prayer or meditation. He's made it. I'm shocked. However, I'm also intrigued and excited as to where we can take this experiment further. This is only the beginning and with further enhancements, there's no telling where the results will end. I imagine this has to be used on our soldiers within ten years. Now, I must release Shekau from the chamber. I'll perform an extensive interview to find out just how the thirty days has affected his mind and body.

Day thirty-one. The gas is shut off and the two guards open the door to go in and release Shekau from his prison. He's serene, almost trance-like as he slowly walks out of the chamber. They lead him to a secluded room on the west side of unit 913. They walk him in and he sits behind a table to wait for Reinheart. All the room contains is the table, two chairs, the door, and a lone window. The sun shines through and Shekau walks over to feel the rays on his face.

Reinheart walks in and watches, as Shekau stands by the window with his eyes closed, feeling the warm goodness of our star.

"Hello, Nasir. How do you feel?"

Shekau turns and looks at the man responsible for his prison for the last thirty days. He smiles and walks over to the chair and sits.

"Once the lingering effects of the gas wear off, you'll become extremely exhausted."

Shekau nods and glares at the scientist.

"I suppose you want to know about your freedom? It's what we agreed on, yes, you to be set free?" Reinheart looked into Shekau's eyes to gauge a reaction but saw nothing.

Shekau waits for Reinheart to continue.

"As soon as this interview is over, you'll get your side of the agreement." Reinheart's eyes quickly dart away. It was just a moment in time. A small reaction that most wouldn't have noticed, but Nasir Shekau is not like most people.

Reinheart smiled. "Now, how was your mind through this experiment?" There is no response and Reinheart clears his throat. "The experiment was never just to break you. You've done the United States military a great service. At what point did you notice a difference?" Shekau still remains silent, continuing his steady gaze.

"How did you stay so calm through everything that happened around you?"

As soon as the sentence was out of his mouth, he grabbed Reinheart by the arm, pulled him forward and impaled Reinheart's right eye with a rib from Hallwell's body, which he spent the last four days sharpening. He walked out of the chamber with it up his sleeve and waited for just the right time to strike. Reinheart screamed in pain as his eyeball exploded and blood flowed freely from the orifice.

"I knew from the beginning you wouldn't let me go. I waited my time, now I take what is mine."

Shekau gets up, kicks Reinheart in the midsection, and uses the chair to smash the lone window. In an instant he is outside, the warm sunshine on his face, running through a field toward the forest-line and his freedom. Reinheart crawls to a button by the door, presses it, and two guards swing the door open and enter.

"Get him! Now!"

The guards run around to the side door that leads to the west field and exit the building. They see Shekau sprinting toward his safety, his deliverance.

"Shoot him, before he gets away!" they hear the doctor yell behind them. They both kneel and take aim with their .50 caliber rifles. Shots ring out into the cool autumn air...

David Boiani

Mexican border, winter, 2016

Nasir Shekau passes over the Mexican border south of Yuma. He isn't sure why he's alive. Whether it was a result of a few bad shots from experienced military shooters, or just pure luck. Maybe the two aimed just a bit north or south of the target because they couldn't bring themselves to end the life of such a brave warrior. The answer is something he'll never know but inside he hopes it's the latter. He won't make his way back to Afghanistan. He knows he'll be tracked down there and possibly given up by his own people.

Lima, Peru. That's where his dreams lead him. Settle down in a small village just outside the city, overlooking the Pacific. Some say the Pacific has no memory, that it forgives and forgets.

Nasir Shekau is banking on that parable.

He continues his path south. Once he's over the border, he's free of any American stronghold. The sun peaks out from behind a few fluffy early morning Mexican clouds and he holds his face to the sky to feel the warm rays. They give him a feeling he hasn't felt in a long time. A feeling like he's just woken after a long slumber. An invigorating, rejuvenating, euphoric feeling.

It's the feeling of freedom.

THE END

AFTERWORD

There are plenty of stories on the internet about governments using prisoners of war for scientific experiments. The rumored Nazi experiments at Auschwitz and other concentration camps included the mutilation of twins, bone, muscle and nerve transplant and regeneration experiments, and induced head trauma tests to deduct how much abuse the human brain can endure. On top of the historical accounts of real experiments, there are numerous fictional stories of macabre practice involving the experimentation and observation of prisoners. Which are real and which are fiction, we may never know. Someday, you just may read a verified account of a so-called Unit 913...

JUST ONE MORE TIME

Just One More Time

I want to feel the unconditional love from my dog's kiss, *just one more time...*

I want to feel the sun's rays on that first beautiful spring day, *just one more time...*

I want to see the brilliant smile on my daughter's face, *just one more time...*

Sometimes we wonder why this world is filled with evil, with uncontrollable darkness...

I want to experience the initial progression of a perfect song, *just one more time...*

I want to hold a newborn baby and feel the innocence, *just one more time...*

I want to smell the crisp scent of a blizzard on the way, *just one more time...*

Sometimes we wonder why we continue, why we fight the darkness and persevere...

I want to achieve something I once thought was impossible, *just one more time...*

I want to gaze at the stars as a warm beach breeze gusts, *just one more time...*

I want to indulge that glass of ice water after an enduring workout, *just one more time...*

But the truth is, nature has a balance. For every darkness, there's a bit of light...

I want to inhale a scent which takes me back to my childhood, *just one more time...*

I want to experience pure laughter that comes from inside, *just one more time...*

I want to hold hands with someone I love, *just one more time...*

For every evil, there's a bit of good...

I want to experience the scent of freshly cut grass, *just one more time...*

I want to feel physical pleasure with a woman, *just one more time...*

I want to read literature that affects me emotionally, *just one more time...*

For every travesty, there's a miracle...

I want to drive with the windows down and my favorite song on the radio, *just one more time...*

I want to witness a stunning sunset with nowhere to be and nothing to do, *just one more time...*

I want to experience true friendship and trust, *just one more time...*

This world isn't filled with only dark, evil and morbid experiences.

Just One More Time

All we have to do is open our senses to what's right in front of us

to experience the bright, good, and joyous...*just one more time...*

About the Author

David Boiani is an American author living in Coventry, RI. He writes Psychological thrillers mixed with a touch of horror. He recently released a collection of short stories called Dark Musings. He is currently writing The Redemption, the sequel to his debut novel, A Thin Line. Visit his website here:

www.authordavidboiani.com

More from David Boiani

Dark Musings
The Redemption
A Thin Line

Other Titles Available from Foundations Book Publishing Company

Dark Musings

By David Boiani

What if real life scenarios were far more horrific than fantasy? What if you could visit the dark, unsettling mind of one man and experience the disturbing stories that originate there? These stories are unconnected, but they all include a similar trait: Fear. They are all based on aspects of life that are haunting yet very real. Experiencing these stories will induce a terror that will stay with you long after the final page is turned...

Farm House

By Steve Soderquist

Ten years ago, a little girl was supposedly murdered. Ten years ago, that little girl got away.

Now after eight years of living on her own, feeding from garbage cans and doing what she must to survive and still remain anonymous, the lies that had been told to her have led her; her sense of vengeance and retribution back to the door-step of whom she considers to blame.

Those who stand in her way receive nothing of mercy, as her relentless pursuit to extract revenge on those who robbed her of her life come to a chilling close as nothing will stop her...and no one is to be spared.

EVIN

By A.S. Crowder

Eva has never seen the Forest of Evin, but her fate and the fate of the Forest may be intertwined.

Sinister forces seek to pull the Forest apart, and Eva may be the only one who can save it. Eva must travel between worlds to keep the Forest together...

...but the Forest of Evin thrums with power and the force tearing it apart may not be the only danger.

Dark Prisoner – The Kruthos Key

By D. Thomas Jerlo

Suna Di'Viao, the last of the Divenean race, has hidden from the world, blaming herself for the demise of King Markes and Queen Saliste.

It's a fate she believes she deserves, but when she's summoned on a quest by a mysterious stranger, her Divenean heritage won't allow her to refuse.

DECEPTION

By Laura Ranger

Izzy's had a lifetime of liars make up her past. All that changes with Caleb Matthews who's genuine and sincere. He teaches her not all is black or white. After 25 years of marriage she begins to suspect there's more to her husband then what she's known. No matter how she tries, she can't find anything amiss.

Is her paranoia from being deceived in her past sabotaging her future or is there something more she's missing?